NICK: FIREBRAND COWBOYS

BARB HAN

TORJAKE PUBLISHING

Copyright © 2023 by Barb Han

All rights reserved.

No part of this book may be reproduced in any form or by any electronic or mechanical means, including information storage and retrieval systems, without written permission from the author, except for the use of brief quotations in a book review.

Editing: Ali Williams

Cover Design: Jacob's Cover Designs

To Brandon, Jacob, and Tori for being the great loves of my life. To Babe for being my hero, my best friend, and my place to call home.

1

Nick Firebrand was about to do something he never believed he'd do in a million years: visit his mother in jail. Jackie Firebrand had been arrested for attempted murder. As far as Nick could tell, she was guilty as sin and not denying her crime.

What the hell was he supposed to do with that?

Thankfully, his twin brother Morgan was beside him and the two of them planned to walk inside together. This was the first time for both of them to darken the door of the county lockup to see a relative. And he could only hope it would be the last time too.

His side of the family had always been the dark sheep of the successful cattle ranching Firebrands. Despite the rumors, he'd been able to hold his head up high when he walked around town because he knew they'd done nothing wrong. Now, the behind-the-back whispers shrouded him in shame. His mother had proven the roots were damaged on this side of the family tree. If anyone had doubted the fact before, her guilt proved it.

"Are you ready for this?" Morgan asked, taking a deep

breath before reaching for the lobby's door handle. The mostly glass and stainless-steel door appeared after hoofing it up thirteen stairs, a baker's dozen, to reach a predominantly non-descript brown-brick, five-story building.

"As ready as I'll ever be," Nick confirmed, which wasn't saying much considering his sour mood and the circumstances surrounding the visit. An unrelated piece of information kept assaulting the back of his mind and ranked right up there with having his mother in jail. Vanessa Mosely was back in town. An old saying came to mind. *Fool me once, shame on you. Fool me twice, shame on me.*

"You first," Nick said to his brother, who was holding the door open.

Morgan gave a quick nod before walking inside. There were no chairs inside the tiled lobby. Video cameras watched over the empty space from every corner where wall met ceiling. A pair of doors opened directly across the lobby, and an officer joined them.

"My name is Sergeant Hopper," the slim, older gentleman with brown hair that was graying at the temples said. "How can I be of service?"

"Nick Firebrand," he said, as he shook the outstretched hand before turning to his brother, who then introduced himself. "We're here to visit Jackie Firebrand." A good son would probably mention the fact she was his mother. Nick couldn't bring himself to. Did that make him a bad person? Maybe. A familial bond wasn't something he'd ever felt with the woman who'd given birth to him. Plus, no one would nominate Nick for sainthood. Did he take after his mother, after all? Did her DNA choke out anything remotely good in him?

No matter how 'out there' the question seemed, it was one of Nick's biggest fears.

The sergeant's expression tightened. "Did an officer reach out to your family?"

"Not that I know of," Nick said, not liking the sergeant's change in attitude. "Why? Did something happen?" He couldn't fathom his mother would be released on bail, considering last he'd heard, the judge refused to set it in order to keep Jackie in county lockup before her trial. He'd argued the family had enough money from the oil rights they'd inherited to not only make bail but help her disappear. No one could argue.

Sergeant Hopper put his hands on his hips and shook his head. "I'm sorry you wasted your time coming here."

"Has she been transported somewhere else?" Nick asked. Last he remembered there'd been talk of moving her to another location. The lawyer she'd hired mentioned it being impossible for her to get a fair trial anywhere near their hometown of Lone Star Pass.

"Yes, sir," the sergeant confirmed. "To the hospital. It seems she received multiple injuries after an altercation with another one of the inmates."

"What the hell happened?" Nick asked as Morgan raked his fingers through his hair and issued a sharp sigh.

When the sergeant hesitated, Morgan cut in, "How bad is it?"

"I apologize for not having all the details of her current condition," the sergeant informed. "It's my understanding there was a disagreement over the meal at lunch. Jailers rushed in as soon as they were alerted to the situation. A group of women locked arms around the fighting inmates, which isn't unusual in these situations, which delayed the guards from separating the females."

Nick noticed the sergeant didn't give so much as a hint as to her well-being. "When can we see her?"

"I'm afraid that's not possible, sir," Sergeant Hopper said. "But you can call this number to receive updates."

The sergeant then provided a number, which both Nick and Morgan entered into their phones.

"I wish I could be more help," Sergeant Hopper conceded with a sigh. "I apologize for you wasting your time and energy coming out to county for me to turn you away."

"Thank you," Morgan said, ever the peacemaker. "We appreciate all that you've done for our mother. Will there be a report about what happened?"

"Working on it now," Sergeant Hopper informed. "Again, my apologies for the lack of notification. We're backed up on paperwork but we'll get the statements into the system as soon as possible."

Nick wasn't so optimistic about the sergeant, whose words didn't match his stern expression. There wasn't a hint of sympathy on a face that seemed made from stone. The fact he did this for a living and had probably seen just about everything could be responsible for the hardened demeanor. Then again, he might not care.

Nick also realized he'd fisted his hands at his sides. He clenched and released his fingers a few times to work off some of the tension. It didn't work.

"Can you tell us what you know so far?" Nick pressed. "You must have been involved in taking statements."

"No, sir," Sergeant Hopper said, standing his ground. "I'm afraid I can't share any information other than what I've already said."

From the point of view of someone on the outside, he could admit, his mother looked like a privileged woman who couldn't wait to get her hands on the bulk of the family fortune. Nick couldn't argue the logic. It made perfect sense. His mother had been a gold digger. No question there. She'd been a trophy wife and would be cast as such in the courts. Courts that would see her with as much disgust as Nick did. She probably deserved every awful thing coming her way. Except one thing, an unfair trial.

Under the circumstances, he didn't believe she would get a fair one.

"What about the warden?" Nick continued. "I'd like to see the person in charge."

"I'm afraid that's not possible at the moment," Sergeant Hopper said. His jaw muscle ticked, which gave Nick the impression the man's patience was running out. "However, I can request an appointment."

Nick knew when he hit a brick wall. The sergeant had no plans to elaborate. It was time to call in the lawyer.

"Call if there's anything else I can help you with," Sergeant Hopper said in a not-so-subtle tone to let them know they were dismissed. More of that judgment clouded the man's eyes as they took Nick and Morgan in, assessing.

He should be used to snap judgments by now; people had been making comments for months about apples never falling far from the tree. So why did it light him up with anger this time?

"We will," Morgan said before ushering Nick to the door.

Outside, Nick couldn't get to his truck fast enough. More of that anger surfaced. Nick needed an outlet before he lost his temper or did something he might not be able to take back.

"Hold on," Morgan said, a few steps behind.

Nick whirled around on his brother, doing his level best to contain his anger.

"What?" Nick asked in as calm a voice as he could muster.

"I don't want you driving off like this," Morgan said. It

was reasonable, except Nick wasn't in the mood for logic when his mother had just been beaten down in jail and was in the hospital.

"Aren't they supposed to protect her in there?" Nick managed to get out through clenched teeth as he paced the length of his truck and back.

"Yes," Morgan said, pulling out his cell phone. "I'm texting our father right now to see if he knows what happened."

Nick hadn't thought about the fact their family group chat hadn't been lighting up. Given this new information, it should be even though every one of his brothers had their own complicated ideas about their mother. No one wanted to see her hurt. Did she need to serve time for the crime she committed? Absolutely. Pay back her debt to society? One hundred percent, yes. Neither of which included being beat up and hospitalized from her injuries.

At that point, he remembered the phone number the sergeant had given them a few minutes ago. Morgan stared at his screen, his toe tapping on the concrete. After a few seconds passed, he shook his head. "No response."

"Let's hope he's on his way to the hospital," Nick said, fishing out his cell. He made a quick call to the number provided and landed in voicemail. Rather than leave a heated message, he ended the call. Nick had learned a long time ago actions made in anger normally came back to bite him in the backside. Hard. In fact, he couldn't think of a time when they'd ever helped a situation. A moment of satisfaction wasn't worth the extra effort it took to repair the damage.

"I doubt they'd let our father see her," Morgan stated. He glanced at his truck. "Why don't you catch a ride with me?

We can grab Avril and then swing by to pick up your truck. She can drive it home while we talk."

His brother's ploy might have worked if Nick was in the mood for company. "I'll take a walk to cool off before I head home."

Morgan didn't look convinced, so Nick threw his hands up in the surrender position.

"I promise not to get behind the wheel while I'm this ticked off," Nick said, trying to allay his brother's fears. Too often someone got behind the wheel after a dust-up and ended up in the hospital or morgue. "I'll go for a walk and cool down."

"Promise?" Morgan asked, knowing full well Nick would stand on his word if he gave it.

Nick held up his right hand, three fingers up and together. "Scout's honor."

The two locked gazes. Morgan gave a slight nod. They'd been able to tell if the other one was lying with shocking accuracy. The twin bond was real, but it hadn't always felt one hundred percent accurate in their case. This time, however, it was dead on.

"Alright," Morgan said before bringing Nick into a bear hug.

"Keep me posted if you hear from him," Nick said, referring to their father.

"Goes without saying," Morgan confirmed. He stood there for a few extra moments. Nick recognized the tactic as buying time. "I better pick up Avril."

"I'm good," Nick said. "Go get her."

Morgan nodded before climbing into his driver's seat and then driving away.

Nick should probably put a message out on the group

chat about what they'd just learned. He bit back a curse. As much as everyone deserved to know what was happening, he couldn't imagine his father finding out that way. He fired off a text to Morgan, asking his brother to give the green light when the news could be sent on the family chat. A personal call seemed better under the circumstances, but he had to admit sending a text was the fastest way to get information out to everyone at one time. They had nine males in the family, so individual communication wasn't always the most efficient.

Morgan's taillights disappeared and, for half a second, Nick considered climbing inside his truck and peeling out of the parking lot. Dammit that he was a man of his word.

Instead, he cut across the street where there was a park. How convenient. The kids of incarcerated criminals could play out here while the other parent went inside for visitation. Was that how it worked? He was too old for a playground but this seemed like a good place to burn off some steam before getting behind the wheel.

"Thought I might run into you at some point," a familiar voice said from behind a tree. She stepped into view. The sunlight from behind cast a halo around her head. But this was no angel.

"What are you doing here, Vanessa?" he bit out. Of course, he would run into her today of all days.

She blinked at him, confused. "It's usual for a litigator to visit her client."

"Her what?" Nick asked. There was no way he'd heard correctly. Because this meant his ex was going to represent his mother.

VANESSA MOSELY almost couldn't believe how good Nick

NICK: Firebrand Cowboys 9

looked standing there with the sun shining on his face. She'd forgotten how good-looking the man was.

"Lawyer," she repeated.

"Why you?" he asked with the kind of bitterness in his tone that said he wasn't happy to see her again. She figured as much. It was too much to ask forgiveness from a stubborn Firebrand, least of all Nick.

"Your mother called in a marker with my father's firm," she said when he didn't continue.

"I remember your situation now," he said, his tone accusing. "Your parents divorced when you were little, and your mother moved to Lone Star Pass to bring you up away from the city."

"Houston doesn't exactly have a lot of skyscrapers, but it does have good lawyers," she quipped defensively. Her father was one of the best defense attorneys in the city. He'd also been her mentor right up until the time he died from a heart attack two months ago. If news of his death had gotten back to Lone Star Pass, Nick seemed to have turned a deaf ear. But then, he probably didn't want to know anything about her or her family after the two of them broke up.

She dropped the cigarette she'd been holding onto the ground and crushed it with the tip of her Manolo Blahnik.

"You don't plan on leaving that there, do you?" he asked with a disgusted look on his face. Nick would never be able to play poker or win in court, considering he wore his emotions on his sleeve. "Because here in the sticks, we call that littering. Not to mention the fact we've been in a drought recently and the sparks from that cigarette could cause the whole county to go up in flames."

She crouched down and picked up the butt. Lighting a cigarette, but not taking a puff, was a habit she'd picked up in law school when overwhelmed with stress. There was something soothing about the faint smell of smoke. It reminded her of the way her father's crisp suits had smelled after a hard day in court. He only smoked during high-profile trials.

Vanessa took a step forward. Getting closer to Nick sent her pulse racing on a track of its own.

"You didn't answer my question," he said.

"I'm certain that I did."

"Why you?" he repeated, like she didn't hear him correctly the first time. Then clarified, "Why isn't your father here? Is my mother's case not worth his time? Or is it just my family that's not worth his time?"

"First of all, my father isn't here because he died a couple of months ago," she said, hearing the catch in her own throat at the word *died*.

Nick opened his mouth to speak, most likely to offer her an apology, but he snapped it shut when she put her hand up.

"Don't," she warned. "You didn't know him and you definitely didn't like him, so you're not sorry."

"I don't have to know him personally to—"

Again, she stopped him cold with that same hand. "We don't have to do this." She made eyes at him. "Play nice." She pinched the cigarette butt in between her thumb and forefinger before flicking it into the nearby trash receptacle. "I'm here to defend your mother. You are part of this case, like it or not, so I'll need to be in contact."

"Sounds like a party," he quipped in the sarcastic tone he'd mastered since the last time they were together. His eyes still held sympathy, though, so she forced her gaze away from his before he got to her. "But what are you doing out here?"

"I was giving you and your brother time with your

mother before I headed inside," she said, lifting her gaze once again to study him. The shift in his tone had her concerned. "I thought you could use some time since I knew you hadn't…"

The way he stared at her caused alarm bells to sound.

"Why? What aren't you telling me, Nick?"

He folded his arms across a broad, muscled chest. "Have you spoken to the desk sergeant today?"

"No, which is why I was about to go inside and do just that," she said, wishing he would get to the point.

"My mother isn't here," he informed. "She was in an altercation with another prisoner earlier today."

"You've got to be kidding me," she said, not bothering to mask her anger. This was turning into a red-letter day.

"Do I look like I would joke about something like this?"

No. He didn't. Dammit.

2

The shock and concern on Vanessa's face was genuine. Nick had witnessed it before. She might have a courtroom face that differed, concealed, but this was not it.

"Why wouldn't her lawyer be notified?" he asked. The phone was already to her ear before Nick could finish his sentence.

"My name is Vanessa Mosely, and I need to know exactly what happened to my client this morning and why I wasn't immediately briefed on the situation," she said in a measured tone. He assumed she spoke to the same disapproving desk sergeant. Hopper.

Nick wouldn't want to be on the other end of the conversation that was about to happen. He also noticed the fact her last name was still Mosely, which didn't mean she wasn't married. She could be using her given name for career purposes. But he couldn't help but glance at her ring finger to confirm her marital status—status that was none of his business. Tell that to his heart. Because the damn thing tried to convince him their history gave him a right to know.

NICK: Firebrand Cowboys 13

Vanessa opened her mouth to speak a couple of times, and then immediately clamped it shut. She huffed out several breaths in a row. If she was a teapot, the whistle was about to blow. She'd earned the fiery reputation most redheads had years back. Good to know some things never change.

"You will give me immediate access to my client and full disclosure of the incident," she finally said with the kind of calm anger that made the earth quake under his boots just a little.

Nick cracked a smile despite the circumstances, which were that his jailed mother had been in an altercation and was presently in the hospital being guarded with a strict no-visitor policy in place. His mind snapped to the possibility she was in surgery or, worse, on life support.

"Oh, I believe you will, sir," she insisted and then proceeded to throw a lot of legal jargon into the conversation. Nick doubted any of it was enforceable, but Vanessa knew how to throw out a threat. The thought of her coming to Lone Star Pass to be his mother's legal counsel sat hard on his mind. There were plenty of other lawyers in Texas. Couldn't his mother have gone to the second name on her list once she found out Theodore Mosely had died?

This also brought up questions as to why his mother knew one of the best criminal defense attorneys in the state. What other crimes had she been committing while she had her freedom? Another darker thought struck about what she'd actually been doing while on her solo weekend trips to Houston. They were supposed to be shopping excursions. Could her word be trusted about any other aspect of her life? Did she know Vanessa's father by reputation or by a personal, more intimate reason?

Of course, now that she was up for attempted murder

charges, there was no going back to an innocent time when he believed her. He might not have respected her but he'd never believed her capable of anything this extreme.

"I have half a mind to file charges against your department for criminal negligence," Vanessa managed to get out through gritted teeth. "You have my information on file, but I can give you my e-mail again if you've misplaced it." Those last words hinted at further incompetence and most likely weren't received well by the sergeant based on her frown. "I have two words for you, Sergeant." She paused for a few seconds. "Try me."

Those must have been the magic words because Vanessa nodded and a satisfied look crossed her features.

"I'll need a tour of the cell my client has been held in," Vanessa continued. "I'm out front right now. I can be inside in less than a minute."

Despite Nick's anger about their past, he couldn't help but be impressed by Vanessa. At least she'd found a positive use for the stubborn streak that had been a mile long when they'd dated. Back then, she'd used it to insist he ask her out. When he'd reminded her that he already had asked her out but she turned him down, she crossed her arms over her chest and told him she would wait right there at his locker until he asked again.

Nick had walked away.

After every class from then on, Vanessa managed to get to his locker before him. On the third day, he broke his own personal policy of never asking someone out twice if he was rejected the first time. Her response?

"I thought you'd never ask."

He should have known she would become a lawyer.

Zoning back into her conversation, he realized she'd ended the call and was studying him.

"He won't give me access yet," she said, impatience edged her tone. The toe tapping didn't help change his opinion. She was wound tighter than ever.

"Did he tell you about the inmates locking arms to make sure the guards couldn't break up the fight right away?" he asked.

She shook her head. "He said there was an accident."

"Bull," Nick said, then repeated the conversation he and Morgan had had with the sergeant.

Vanessa seethed. She opened her mouth to speak.

The crack of a bullet split the air, the echo almost deafening. Instinct kicked in as Nick dove toward Vanessa. The ping of a bullet hitting the metal trash can, not five feet away from them, would have sobered a drunk.

"Stay down," he whispered in Vanessa's ear as he covered her with his body, ignoring the whiff of spring flowers and clean skin that assaulted his nostrils...her scent. His pulse kicked up a few more notches as adrenaline mixed with a sudden hit of desire.

"I won't move except to call the desk sergeant back," she quickly said, fear in the tone that, moments ago, had sounded so confident. The fact she had to be scared at all filled him with rage.

Someone had a lot of nerve shooting at them across the street from the jail. The main reason the shooter missed was most likely that he was shooting out of range. It was windy, and the shooter must not have been experienced enough to calculate the impact wind had at a distance. Or else, they did have experience and flat-out missed. It happened.

Nick scanned the area behind where he'd been standing, searching for any signs of movement. Thankfully, they'd been standing in a relatively open space. The bullet would have to have traveled a long distance to reach them, and that was most likely the only reason they were both intact and not bleeding out with a GSW.

Vanessa barely had the phone to her ear when a couple of men in full-on law enforcement gear along with bulletproof vests came running toward them, rifles in position and ready.

"Are you injured?" one of the officers asked.

"No, sir," Nick responded, his mind sifting through anyone who might try to shoot him in broad daylight in front of county lockup.

The people in SWAT gear fanned out. "Stay down until we've secured the area."

"Yes, sir," Nick stated. He had no intention of getting in the way of law enforcement officers, despite having to fight every instinct to hop to his feet and join them while they searched for the bastard responsible for the bullet. Five feet was all that stood between the two of them and a direct hit.

Underneath him, he could almost feel Vanessa's heart beating wildly. His muscles corded with tension at being so close to her that he could breathe in her clean and jasmine-like scent. His body betrayed him as his throat dried up and his stomach free-fell. She was a beautiful woman with whom he'd been head over heels in love with at one point in time. His reaction probably shouldn't surprise him as much as it did.

Shoving those thoughts aside, he refocused on the fact someone had tried to kill them a couple of minutes ago.

After what felt like an eternity but was probably four or five minutes, someone said, "All clear."

Nick pushed to standing and then offered a hand to Vanessa, which she accepted. The second bare skin touched, electricity was a lightning bolt up his arm. His fingers pulsed, then his arm, his shoulder, and then a line straight to his heart. It was like static electricity when it struck, causing his pulse to thunder inside his ribcage.

"We're okay?" Vanessa asked, her vulnerable voice another shot to the heart.

Without thinking, Nick looped his arms around her waist and hauled her against his chest. Her hands came up to his shoulders. For a split-second, he thought she might push him away. And then, her nails dug into him like she needed an anchor.

"You're fine," he said as he pulled back, realizing those words under different circumstances would have a very different subtext. For now, it worked and fit the current situation. There would be no mistaking their meaning.

She rewarded him with a genuine heart-melting smile. "Thank you. I don't know what would have happened if you hadn't been here."

"You probably would have been better off," he countered.

"Why would you think that let alone say it?" she asked, cocking her head to one side as she stared up at him.

"We have no idea who the shooter was going for," he clarified. "And it very likely could have been me."

VANESSA HADN'T STOPPED LONG ENOUGH to consider the possibility someone was coming after Nick. As a defense lawyer, she assumed the bullet had been meant for her. "I'm pretty sure I'm the target here, Nick" She shook her head. "It was stupid of me to come here alone without some kind of security. This is a high-profile case. I should have known better."

The other problem was that her dad had made a lot of

money but he spent it just as fast. Two months had passed and the pain was still just as raw as when she'd first learned of her father's heart attack. She missed him from somewhere deep. He wasn't perfect. Even she knew about his flaws, but he was her father. He'd loved her in his own way and looked out for her. He was larger than life, and she would miss that. Without his presence, it was like someone sucked all the air out of the room at the law firm.

She feared his addictions got the best of him, and everyone was about to pay the price. The man had had a gambling addiction the size of Texas, and that was saying something. The recent visit she had last week from someone who went by the name Trash Collector had scared the bejesus out of her and opened her eyes to how bad her father's gambling had become.

The tall, black-haired man who looked to be in his late thirties had some kind of Rocky Balboa fixation based on the way he spoke and the gray jogging suit he wore. She negotiated for more time, and he'd agreed. Could the bullet have been a warning shot? Trash Collector came across as the type to want up-close contact. There were other threats that came across her desk. Ones with cutout letters on paper to mask handwriting. They were creepy. She kept those in her purse, just in case. And then there were the endless verbal threats that came with the job from people who believed her clients shouldn't get away with their crimes. The religious zealots could be frightening. A few cases stayed with her. The ones involving abused wives or having children pulled from their homes. Advising on domestic violence cases might be gratifying but they came with risk.

Either way, the shooter was most likely tied to money owed. A successful high-profile case meant she would be able to pay off debt and get the firm in the black again.

"I'm here," Nick said in a voice that sounded put off.

"By sheer accident," she reminded him. "This situation could have been a whole lot worse if you hadn't been."

"As much as I want to believe what you're saying could be true," he started. "I can't risk it. My family has been through too much recently to ignore this. Until we find out who the shooter is after and why, you just found a new sidekick."

Vanessa's heart squeezed at the thought of spending time with Nick. Had she secretly hoped they would run into each other while she was in town? Yes. Of course, she was going to interview him for her client's case, but she'd hoped the first time they saw each other again would be under better circumstances. A grocery run-in. Or at the gas station. Something to break the ice so she could gauge where they stood before she had to call on him officially, which would have been soon because she needed to find a way to get her client released from jail.

The shooter incident gave her ammunition to work with while Jackie Firebrand was in the hospital to endure her client never came back to this county lockup. But there was no way she wanted things to go down like this, including her first meeting with Nick.

"We can talk as much as you want, but I'd get a dog if I wanted constant company," she said, needing to keep a healthy distance between her and Nick. Even after all these years, he had a unique ability to disarm her. Being near him made her lifestyle feel lacking. So what if she'd stayed home every Friday night for the past year? Or more. There was nothing wrong with having a movie night in the comfort of her PJs and overstuffed sofa. So what if she'd spent those evenings alone, along with a whole heap of Saturday nights too? Nick had her wishing for better options.

But right now, all she could afford to focus on was her client.

A lawman walked straight up to them and then introduced himself as Sergeant Hopper. She sized him up as someone who looked invested in his job. The wedding band said he was married. The slight beer belly said he probably sat around and watched football when he was off duty when it was in season. If she had to guess, he most likely had two kids, older. Maybe teenagers. The fact he had no sunburn, meaning he didn't spend his time off standing outside to watch his kid play baseball or football, caused her to guess daughters. Being able to read people had always been a strong suit for Vanessa. The skill had been honed by trial experience. She'd had to figure out jury members based on how they looked as they filed in for jury duty. Of course, she also got to read their files, but correct split-second impressions were her best weapon. Her instincts honed by experience were making her one of the best up-and-coming lawyers in Houston. Her plan to one-day sit on the opposite side of the desk could still be in reach if she kept up this pace—a pace that had caused her social life to become anemic.

She also could use a case with notoriety under her belt, a high-profile case like Jackie Firebrand's. With so many eyes on her, the pressure was real and she had to win. She didn't have her father's inclination toward risking it all or throwing her chips into a high-stakes game, but making him proud had taken on a whole new meaning since his death. After learning of his gambling addiction, the halo she'd always seen around his head started to lose its shine.

"Also, you have no idea how many folks out there might not want your mother to receive fair representation," she continued, jumping back into the conversation with Nick.

"So, unless someone's been taking shots at you lately, this was probably all about me signing on to the case."

"Why didn't she call you when this first started?" he asked.

Vanessa couldn't believe Nick was so clueless as to what was going on with his mother's case. "Don't you read the news?"

"I try to avoid it actually," he said in a judgmental tone.

She would deal with that later. "Your mother's attorney withdrew from the case. He was going to leave her up to a public defender now that your father planned to cut her off financially."

"Cut her off?" Nick repeated. He really was in the dark about his mother's situation. The realization shouldn't catch her off guard. She'd dated Nick, been to his home. He'd never been close to either one of his parents and had never seemed to mind. To be honest, she always admired the way his folks never got under his skin. It had been so easy for him to walk away and ignore pretty much everything going on at home.

"That's right," she said. "No more money from Firebrand coffers. I'm sorry for being the one to tell you. I thought maybe you already knew or that it was a family decision."

He shook his head. "My family is even more messed up than they were before."

Vanessa reached out and touched his forearm. "I'm sorry, Nick. I didn't realize how much worse it must have gotten for you."

Nick took a step back, breaking contact. It was probably for the best, considering how her skin reacted to touching him, not to mention the dozen campfires that lit inside her every time they stood close to each other. Still, the move hurt her feelings. Since he wasn't the type to hurt someone on purpose, she tried to brush it off. "I'm not the one you need to worry about."

"Okay," she said. "That's fair. But I do need you to be able to talk about your mother and your home life in front of a jury without coming across so angry."

Nick just stared at her for a long moment.

"You don't get it, do you?" he finally asked.

"Get what, Nick?"

"The fact my mother is guilty."

"Allegedly—"

"Don't tell me that she's changing her plea," he said, raking his fingers through his hair.

"I'm trying to talk her into it," she said as she studied him.

"Do you believe she's innocent?" he asked, challenging her.

"I believe in justice and receiving a fair trial," she countered.

Nick started to pace. His anger was a slow boil just like she remembered. "You can forget me stepping into any courtroom and pretending to be a family that we aren't. In fact, you might want to leave me completely out of the process considering the fact I'll only hurt your case because I won't lie to a jury."

"No one is asking you to," she said.

"You sure about that?"

"Nick," she started, but the question died on her tongue. The other thing she was really good at was knowing when a battle had been lost. "Okay, I won't ask you to go to court or step in on behalf of your mother in any way." She put her hands up defensively. "I wouldn't ask you to do anything that made you uncomfortable or say anything that is untrue.

Period." She stood there, waiting for a response. None came. "Deal?"

"In exchange for what?" he asked.

"Nothing," she said, confused as to why he asked.

"Then, why did you just ask me to make a deal?"

"I meant that figuratively," she informed, figuring he was in no mood to give her a break. The reunion she'd hoped for wasn't happening. Looking back on their past, forgiveness was probably too much to ask. "But right now, I have to go to the hospital to check on your...*my* client. If you plan to be my shadow, you better hop to it."

Instead of standing there and waiting for a rebuttal, she turned toward the parking lot and headed toward her sedan.

"Hold on," Nick said, but she just kept walking, because if she stopped and looked back at him, she might find herself falling for him all over again.

3

Nick tucked his pride down deep and followed Vanessa to her sedan. He needed to see her to her car in part to make sure she was okay. It was easy to see fear in those blue eyes that were normally so clear they were like looking at the Caribbean Sea. The shot that had been fired had set her nerves on edge, which was understandable. Her reasons for believing the bullet was meant for her were as solid as his own. Time would tell who was right.

Vanessa stopped cold, just shy of reaching the door of her gray sedan. "On second thought, can you drive?"

A retort came to mind but he canned it. Maybe the sarcasm would work another time. Plus, he'd already shown too much of his hand when it came to being off due to seeing her again. "Yes. I'm able to drive."

"We're going to the same place, and it would give me a chance to work on the way," she said.

Multitasking. The true hallmark of an overachiever. But then, Vanessa had always been one of the smartest, most motivated students he'd ever known. In high school, he'd admired her determination. And then he'd resented it for being one of the reasons she'd walked out on him when he'd been in love with her. They were feelings he'd been naïve enough to believe were reciprocal.

"I'm parked over this way," he said, heading toward his truck across the lot. For a split-second, he considered asking how she knew he was the one trying to visit his mother, but then he saw the Firebrand logo on the back window of his pickup. That explained how she knew a Firebrand was here. With eight brothers and nine cousins, how did she know who the vehicle belonged to?

He opened the passenger door before she climbed inside. She had a strap on her shoulder belonging to her oversized, overstuffed handbag and another that looked like it held a laptop and notepads. Both looked heavy, like she could use them to curl if there were no dumbbells available. Who knew what else she carried inside those bags? A gun might have been helpful a little while ago, but she wouldn't bring one of those to jail since it was prohibited and would set off the metal detector.

Nick reclaimed the driver's seat as Vanessa unburdened herself from the heavy bags. Her confidence about the shooter had been niggling at the back of his mind. He started the engine and then backed out of the parking spot. "What makes you so certain the shooter is after you and not me?"

From the corner of his eye, he saw her shake her head.

"I'm an attorney, which people hate," she said. "I always assume the worst until proven otherwise."

"You have that backward, by the way," he pointed out.

"No, I don't," she countered, not looking up from her phone screen. "A judge and jury have to look at a suspect as innocent until proven guilty. That's the court's responsibility.

A defense attorney might have to convince themselves their client is innocent in order to defend them, but they assume the person is guilty while building a case."

"You learn that in law school?" he asked. It sounded backward but he understood the necessity.

"No," she said. "My father. He taught me the ropes before..." She turned her face to the window. He assumed the move was meant to hide the sudden bout of emotion. Vanessa had always been tough, even back in the day. Except with him. There were times when she let her guard down and let him in. That was the good stuff that made him fall head over heels for her. The vulnerable side that she only showed to him.

"I'm sorry for your loss," Nick said. He might not have been a fan of Theodore Mosely, but that didn't mean he wished the man harm. What he remembered most about the person was how stressed out he made his daughter. There were the usual grade standards that were near impossible to meet in an academically rigorous program chosen by him. Vanessa had no choice but to follow his rules, or she would have to move in with him in Houston, which had ended up happening anyway because Mr. Mosely couldn't have his daughter dragged down by the likes of Nick. The other demands he'd made had been significant. She had to graduate a year early while taking college-level classes during her junior and senior years of high school. Then, she had to do undergrad in three years so she could start law school at twenty. Then there were extracurriculars. Her mother had been run ragged driving her daughter back and forth to Houston so she could participate in homeschool debate teams. Mr. Mosely had arranged with the local high school to allow Vanessa to use the swimming pool for her training because Ivy League schools liked versatile students.

When the time had come to graduate, Nick had set his pride aside and offered an alternate scenario. One where the two of them stayed together because he'd been certain she was the one and he'd never find another person who fit him quite like she did. He'd been a damn fool.

Vanessa said she couldn't let her dad down. Her parents had been high school sweethearts too. Her mother had worked to put her father through law school. They'd had a baby girl once he finished. And then, the two tried to stay together for the sake of the baby. As long as Vanessa could remember, her parents fought. Bad fights that sometimes ended with her mother being shoved into the wall. Her father had moved to Houston to open his law practice and her mother had returned to Lone Star Pass, where she'd grown up. Work seemed to keep Mr. Mosely from meeting his commitment to drive to Lone Star Pass to pick up his daughter. And then work seemed to take over all his free time, but he still managed to keep the demands on his daughter sky-high. Vanessa had a blind spot when it came to her father. The man could do no wrong.

One Friday night, Nick came over to find Vanessa holding her mother on the couch not long after they'd settled into their new home in Lone Star Pass. Her mother was curled up like a child, sobbing. As it turned out, divorce papers had come that day. Her mother never spoke about what sparked the breakup, but he assumed whatever happened had been the final straw in a relationship that had long been dead.

It wasn't until years later he learned that her mother had walked into the law office that her blood, sweat, and tears had helped build to find her husband on his paralegal. Literally. The ultimate betrayal.

"I know you didn't care much for him," Vanessa finally said.

"Can't say that I knew him personally," he admitted. He didn't like the way Vanessa changed when she came back from Houston holiday visits with her father. Her walls came up every time and they'd become more and more difficult to break down again. Not to mention the fact her father had been the one to break up Nick and Vanessa's relationship. So, no, he didn't like Theodore Mosely. Finding out he was a cheat didn't make him more popular with Nick either.

"It was my decision, not his," she said so quietly he almost didn't hear.

"Glad we cleared that up. It's ancient history as far as I'm concerned," he bit out. "I see no reason to dredge up the past. Do you?"

"No," she said without enthusiasm. Besides, the admission didn't make him suddenly like her father. "He had problems."

"Doesn't everyone?"

"Yes, but I'm talking about serious ones," she said as her cell buzzed. She muttered a curse and then sent a text. "But that was while he was alive, so..."

There seemed to be a bigger story lurking, but he didn't want to know about Theodore Mosely's problems when Nick had a few of his own. Namely, his mother's recent injuries. He wouldn't be human if he wasn't worried about what happened. So, he changed the subject because the last thing he wanted to do was discuss a man he never respected and only knew of by reputation. "Any word on my mother's condition?"

If shifting the conversation bothered her, she didn't show it. But then, she would have made an excellent poker player. She had a tell but he was driving and couldn't see her face.

"Nothing yet," she said. "Other than the fact I've been reassured she is alive."

That was more than he knew five minutes ago. "No word on how it started or who else might be involved?"

She shook her head as she turned to face the window a second time. This time, she brought her hand up to her face, drumming her fingers on her chin. "We'll find out what happened. I won't stop until we know the truth and folks are held accountable." He could have sworn he heard her add, "I owe you that much."

VANESSA HOPED she could make good on the promises she'd just made. Nick deserved that much, at least. She fired off a text to Sergeant Hopper requesting that report ASAP. On a sharp sigh, she pushed away the thoughts about who might be trying to shoot her and refocused on Nick. "Tell me everything you know about your mother's case."

"I know she's guilty," he said with something that sounded a lot like remorse in his tone.

"What makes you so sure?" she asked, curious to hear his reasoning

"It's been all but proven," he said. "She confessed and admitted guilt. What else do you need?"

"Didn't someone else come after Morgan recently?" she asked. "Like super recently."

"Yes," he admitted. "Decker Gambit, a former ranch hand who claimed my mother promised to cut him into the profits if he aided her. What does he have to do with my mother's innocence?"

"It's possible your mother was covering for someone else," she said.

He shook his head. "No."

"What makes you so certain?" she continued.

"A direct confession from—"

"You mean coercion?" she asked, pushing the issue while cutting him off. If she could plant seeds of doubt in his head when he'd been convinced of his mother's guilt, she could definitely do the same with a jury. Throwing herself into work helped ease some of the ache of losing her father. And in a small way, she felt more connected to him while she was working despite those early days when going into the office made her legs feel like rubber bands. Despite his imperfections—and there'd been plenty—she missed him.

"Lawler is a good sheriff," Nick said.

"What makes you say so?" she continued, trying to rattle him.

"His track record, for one," he said without missing a beat. "She was caught in the act. Or haven't you read the arrest file?"

Vanessa would have to overcome her client being inside the van outside the victim's house that proved she was there. Good. This was exactly the kind of material she needed to uncover. She had to find the biggest objections first so she could poke holes in the district attorney's case. Then, she could focus on the small details of the case against her client. "I have. Were you there?"

"No," he said with disdain in his voice. "I wouldn't want to be, either."

"Then, you can't say for certain what happened," she pointed out, testing the water with his patience.

NICK: Firebrand Cowboys   31

Nick got quiet. Real quiet. The kind of quiet calm that came right before severe weather.

Vanessa decided not to push him. Not yet. She'd gained valuable information from him that would be on everyone else's mind too. The confession. Being caught at the scene. She exhaled and then pinched the bridge of her nose to stave off the headache trying to form at the point right between her eyes.

Since this wasn't a good time to talk, she checked her cell phone to see if the report had come through. Granted, the sergeant wouldn't want to release it to an attorney without it being thoroughly checked over for accuracy. Depending on what happened in the jail, Vanessa might be able to request her client be moved to a mental institution for her own safety. Being accused of murder in these parts didn't make for a safe stay in jail. Plus, she'd already filed a motion to have the case moved to a bigger city. There, she would get a more sympathetic jury pool. It was always the case with larger cities, which made Houston a great place to set up a criminal defense law practice. Her father's plans to open a Dallas office for her to head up once she was established would never bear fruit now that he was gone. Besides, the firm's balance sheet needed reconciling before she could even think about doing anything else. The money problems hit hard again. She was in a hole she had no idea how to dig out of if this case didn't help.

Without her father, the dream felt hollow.

"I have ibuprofen in the gym bag behind your seat," Nick said, his voice cutting through her heavy thoughts.

"I don't have any water," she said.

"Water's in the bag," he said, nodding his head toward the seat.

Vanessa reached behind and located the handle. With

some finagling, she managed to pull the heavy bag up and over. In times like these, she decided to renew her gym membership so she could lift weights and become stronger. Grabbing a bag and lifting it shouldn't be so hard.

The items were there, just like he'd said. "Mind if I take one of these power bars? I just realized I've had three cups of coffee and no breakfast."

"Take whatever you need," he said, his masculine voice unreadable as he navigated off the highway. Hospital signs pointed the way, but she knew this area by heart. She'd grown up in Lone Star Pass and, at one time, wished she could spend her whole life here.

Things changed. People changed. Times changed.

"Do you need one?" she asked.

"I'm good."

She used to be able to read him better. Now, she wasn't sure if he really meant those words. "Are you sure?"

"I'll survive," he said with a nod.

She opened a bar, sliding the wrapper down halfway so he could eat while he drove, and then held it out toward him. After a few quiet seconds, he reached for the protein bar. Next, she opened a bottle of water and set it in the console cup holder.

"That's for you," she said before opening one for herself. Not a minute later, both were empty and more than her stomach felt satisfied.

"I didn't realize how much I needed to get something in my stomach," he said. "Thank you."

This was a start. Could she build on it?

"For what it's worth, I'm sorry about what happened to your mother today," she started. "No matter how much she hurt you in the past and with her actions, this must feel awful that you're out here and she's in there."

His grip tightened on the steering wheel, so she figured she'd gone as far as she could with the conversation about his emotions.

Could she get him to tell her what he knew about the case? "I'd like to hear your side of what happened to land your mother behind bars. If that's okay with you."

"You heard my take on the situation," he said through clenched teeth.

Vanessa needed an angle. She needed something to explain why a mother was so distant from her son. "Then, tell me about your relationship with her."

"I won't testify in court to try to get her off for committing a crime she's guilty of," he countered. "And I have no plans to help you with her defense in any way, shape, or form, even if she is my mother. I believe in justice and the fact that no one should be above the law even when it hits this close to home."

At least she knew where Nick stood. And, no, he wasn't going to be any help to her case.

Could she get sympathy with the court from the violent attack?

"Also, she probably provoked the other inmate," Nick stated. "My mother has never been good at holding her tongue with criticism. I'm guessing she picked on the wrong person."

If that was true, Vanessa's work was cut out for her. They were about to find out.

4

Nick meant his words. He had no plans to aid his mother's attorney in getting her a lighter sentence or cleared of charges. Jackie Firebrand was caught red-handed. She admitted to attempted murder. She tried to cajole his grandfather into reallocating his fortune so she benefited. Not only were her actions illegal but they were just plain underhanded. As much as he wished none of this was real, facts were facts.

An ambulance screamed past as Nick pulled over to the side of the road. "You've been checking your phone a lot. I'm guessing there's still no word on my mother's condition or you would have said something. Right?"

"I'm afraid I don't have anything to report back yet," Vanessa said with compassion. Despite her tough exterior, there was a soft person in there. At least, there used to be. He had no idea what she was like now. Given how high and thick the walls constructed between them were, he figured she intended to keep it that way. "I'm really sorry about that, Nick." She went back to her cell phone's screen before typing out a message. "Maybe this one will get attention."

"We're about to find out for ourselves," he said as he pulled into the hospital parking lot.

"There could be other reasons for the attack," Vanessa said quietly.

"Like?"

"Someone could be threatening your mother to stay quiet," she pointed out.

He nodded as he pulled into a parking spot. "We already know she was the mastermind behind it all. What else could there be?" Nothing could redeem his mother's actions in his eyes. She'd crossed a line no one should. There was no going back now.

"I'm spitballing here," she admitted. "But your mother wouldn't have called me in to defend her if there wasn't a reason for me to be here."

"The reason is to get her off scot-free," he quipped, pulling into a parking spot. He let the engine idle for a long moment while they sat in silence. "Why did you really take the case?"

"What's that supposed to mean?"

She could be defensive until the cows came home. This case was a slam dunk for any halfway decent DA. Why would she take on something so unwinnable?

And then the reason dawned on him.

"How's your career going?" he asked. He could do a little research and find out for himself but figured he could ask while he had her in the truck.

"What's that supposed to mean?" she asked, indignant. Her response told him everything he needed to know.

He cut off the engine. "Chase any ambulances lately?"

Vanessa was out the passenger side before he could round the front of his vehicle. "If you're asking me if I came looking for this? The answer is no. Your mother reached out and..." her blue eyes flashed anger. "I thought I would try to help for old times' sake. Figured I owed you one, but I can see that you have no intention of letting go of the past." She stomped right past him toward the white brick hospital building. "Plus, no one else was going to take a case that, like you said, is a slam dunk. And I thought your mother deserved a fair chance at a legal defense."

Nick muttered a string of curse words. He owed her an apology after speaking before he engaged his brain. Accusing her of being predatory was a jerk move. For now, he would table the apology and see how the rest of the day panned out. Vanessa wouldn't accept it right now anyway. She had too much pride. The notion she would come back to Lone Star Pass to give his mother a fighting chance *for him* was the last thing he expected Vanessa Mosely to say. It caught him off guard. He refused to let it soften his stance toward her, though. This seemed like a good time to remind himself that a good attorney figured out what someone wanted to hear and fed it to them. Right?

As much as he didn't buy this as the case with Vanessa, it was easier to swallow than her carrying around remorse all these years. Even so, it hit him square in the chest.

Following a couple of steps behind, he tucked his cell phone inside his pocket. The group chat message he would like to send about what happened earlier would have to wait. On second thought, what if the bullet had been meant for him? What if others in the family were at risk?

Fishing the cell out, he palmed it as the double glass doors swished open. Rather than get the whole family riled up by firing off a text about a shooter, he told everyone to use extra caution and stay on alert. A reminder not to let their guard down was always a good idea. He followed up by saying he would explain later and then requested a family meeting. Vanessa had said so herself, she would need to talk to the family. This was the easiest way to get it done.

By the time they reached the elevator, his phone started blowing up with questions. While they waited for the ding, he reassured the group he was alive and well.

Morgan called.

"Hey, I'm about to get in an elevator, so we might get cut off," Nick answered.

"Everything okay?" Morgan asked.

"There was an incident outside at the park across the street from the jail after you left," Nick explained as the ding sounded. "I'm safe. Just be careful."

Morgan muttered a curse. He, of all people, would be sensitive about an attack; especially after what he'd just been through with the former ranch hand their mother had promised to split the inheritance money with. "Do you think there could be more folks involved?"

"We'll see," Nick said as he stepped inside the metal cage. He wasn't claustrophobic but he sometimes questioned engineering skills. This space appeared to be sound, if slow. At least he didn't lose the call with his brother.

"Rowan won't be at the meeting you called," Morgan continued.

"Did he say why not?" Nick asked, before he realized not enough time had passed for Rowan to have had a conversation with Morgan about his whereabouts.

"He's gone," Morgan said. "Said something about being fed up with all this nonsense. Said he was heading to Colorado to do some camping. Who knows where he is. That was yesterday. I dropped by last night to see if he was serious but his place was dark."

"Might do some good for him to get away," Nick said,

thinking he should probably do the same. He glanced over at Vanessa, who was staring at her screen.

"I guess," Morgan said. "I just don't like the idea of any of us being on our own right not."

"Understandable," Nick replied. "What about the others?"

"Everyone's in and out," Morgan said. "You know how it is around here. Getting everyone in the same room is about as easy as herding cats."

"We all have our own lives," Nick admitted but it was much more than that. The family was divided once again.

"Where are you now?" Morgan asked.

"You'll never believe this," Nick said.

"Try me."

"I'm with Vanessa Mosely at the hospital," Nick informed.

Another string of swear words filled the line. "Are you serious? What are you doing with her?" And then it must have dawned on Morgan. "Her father is a defense attorney, isn't he?"

"Was," Nick clarified. "He passed a couple of months ago."

Morgan sucked in a breath. "Are you telling me that his daughter is our mother's new attorney?"

"That's right," Nick said, muting his own reactions to his brother's epiphanies. "She's right here if you have any specific questions."

"Got it," Morgan said, clearly taking the hint. "I'll save mine for when I see you both later. I'm assuming she is the reason you've called the family together."

"It'll be easier for her to speak to all of us at once," Nick said. Although, all nine of them could be overwhelming. Then, there were his cousins, all of whom had settled down

NICK: Firebrand Cowboys 39

in a manner of months. It was wild when he really thought about all nine of them discovering their forever people when he couldn't be further from wanting or needing the same. Even Morgan and two of their other brothers were married or planning weddings. The joke about there being something in the drinking water at the ranch was growing old. The only thing in that water was rust from old pipes.

"I'll see what I can do about rounding up the others," Morgan promised. "Does she want our cousins involved?"

"She'll have to tackle that side on her own," Nick said. It was still a sore and uncomfortable subject between cousins for obvious reasons. Nick was surprised it didn't divide them again, but everyone seemed intent on trying to glue the family back together after all the recent tragic events. Not to mention the fact their grandfather, the one responsible for creating the divide in the first place, was gone. Nick's mother had found out their grandfather had planned to cut them out of the will in order to leave money to his mistress. It was a mess. The fallout from one man's life and machinations was still being felt like waves of sound in a canyon.

The elevator dinged, indicating they'd stopped on his mother's floor.

"I have to go," he said into the phone before ending the call with a promise to report back immediately.

With no information, Nick feared he was about to walk into another mess.

∼

TWO PRISON GUARDS approached the minute the doors opened. Vanessa held up a hand to stop them. "I'm the attorney of record for Mrs. Firebrand. I have a right to visit with my client."

"I need to see some ID," one of the guards said. His nametag read: Wilton. He was roughly six feet tall, with buck teeth, and a big nose. He wore his hair in a comb-around. The fluorescent lighting bounced off the crown of his head.

Vanessa dug into her bag, located her wallet after some digging—she really needed to clean that thing out—and then produced her driver's license.

"Ma'am, this license expired last month," he said after staring at the date.

She bit back a curse. Of course, it had. She'd been swimming in paperwork and e-mails. She remembered something coming through but forgot all about the notice while she grieved her father. Her grief was being cut short since saving the law firm and preserving his legacy had to take center stage. Besides, lawyers were threatened all the time. Sometimes directly and some of the threats were veiled. It came with the territory and was part of the not-so-glamorous side of her job—a job that had felt lackluster until Jackie Firebrand called asking for help.

Vanessa issued a sharp sigh. "Is it still within the grace period?"

"Technically—"

"Then, I suggest you allow me access to my client," she said, cutting the guard off and taking control of the situation. The term *fake it till you make it* applied here. She'd noticed the person who seemed like they had the most authority in a given room was the one everyone listened to.

Wilton studied her for a moment before rechecking the ID. He handed it back with a nod. "Right this way, ma'am."

It wasn't a good sign that she still hadn't received a full report from the sergeant. What was he trying to cover up? Incompetence? Or something bigger? A high-profile case like this one could attract a lot of attention. She wondered how Nick would feel if Vanessa ramped up news coverage on the case. If she 'leaked' a few tidbits of information, could she cause the stir she needed to get the trial relocated if the altercation wasn't evidence enough?

Would Nick object to the plan? The last thing she wanted to do was cause him more pain. Could she afford to care about his opinion? Another thought hit harder. This was a big case. The stakes were high. Was Vanessa up to the job? In theory, she knew all the correct steps to take. Reality was a whole other beast. Right now, she couldn't afford to doubt herself.

Doing what was best for her client had to come first. She had to do what was right and not worry about sparing anyone else's feelings. The first rule of a good defense attorney was staying emotionally detached even if her heart protested after seeing the pain in his eyes.

"Hold on there, sir," the second guard said to Nick. "You need to stay out here."

"He's with me," Vanessa stated, taking a step back as Nick squared off with the guard. The determination in Nick's expression said he would walk right through the guard if he tried to stop him. "Hey, hey." The looks between the two men could melt a glacier. "I said he's with me."

"Last I checked, only an attorney had the right to see a client," the man said, digging his heels in.

"I'd be happy to file an injunction against you," Vanessa stated. "Or how about I just call your boss right now and get his clearance." She didn't think the sergeant would green light Nick going into his mother's room, but she said the words with the kind of authority few folks challenged in her experience. Plus, she had an ace in the hole. Her uncle was the warden. The two of them weren't exactly close but she could play the card and bluff her way through if she had to.

The guard studied her before checking with his partner. The two conferred for a few seconds before green-lighting the entry.

"I'd like to speak to my client's doctor," she said to the nurse's station as they were escorted past. Nick walked a step behind, and she could feel the tension radiating from him. Without any idea of the condition of his mother, they were walking in blind. Meaning, she had no idea what to expect. Her lawyer instincts were probably kicking in because she wanted to prepare Nick for what he might encounter. But he was grown and would be quick to remind her of the fact if she forgot.

Still, she slowed her pace and reached for his forearm. The touch, meant to offer reassurance, sent a firebolt of electricity rocketing through her. Based on his reaction, the same thing happened to him. Though, neither would admit as much to each other.

All these years later, and the chemistry they'd shared still sizzled.

Even though this—whatever *this* was—fell into the category of 'never gonna happen,' it was good to know it still existed in the general sense. Why hadn't she felt this way in far too long?

First of all, she'd graduated high school early. Secondly, she'd done undergrad in three years. Don't even get her started on law school. Despite taking all three years to finish, the workload at University of Texas at Austin Law was more than enough to kill any social life. She'd dated a couple of study buddies, mainly because those were the only other humans she knew, but nothing serious had ever come of the short relationships. She'd told herself stress had slaughtered romance, but it was more like lack of interest on her part. The heartbreak after walking away from Nick had been soul-crushing, and her fault. Being young and naïve, she didn't realize what they'd found in each other was rare.

Vanessa needed more than another pretty face to light the kind of campfires inside her that Nick had no trouble doing. She was much more attracted to what was 'under the hood' so to speak, namely, a guy's brain. The way a person looked at life and what they liked to talk about was far more important than outwardly physical good looks.

Although, it didn't hurt that Nick's made her stomach flip-flop like a dozen butterflies had been released inside her. He was pretty to look at. He would also laugh at being described as pretty. But there was no denying the adjective fit.

He cut her off at the door of his mother's room.

"Hold on a second," he said with a concerned look—a look that stopped her in her tracks.

5

"What is it, Nick?"

Vanessa's clear blue eyes coupled with the concern in her expression reached a place deep inside. Nick decided it was best not to dwell on physical reactions, especially like the ones that happened every time they made physical contact.

"Do you want to wait here and let me go in first?" he asked, figuring he could spare her from a horrific scene if his mother was in bad shape.

"I could ask the same question to you," she said. "But I won't because I know there's nothing that would stop you from turning around and walking inside that door."

Nick agreed. He didn't want to go into detail about the fact his mother could be faking the whole fight scenario. It was possible she wasn't even injured but came up with a plot to get out of jail for a little while. She had to realize she'd be sent back but maybe saw this as a break or mini vacation. The woman had nearly pulled off a murder plot, so there was that to consider. When it came to her mind, he didn't rule anything out.

His thoughts bounced between fearing she had crossed a line with another inmate, causing a fight that she would certainly lose, and her faking it. It was a sad statement that he couldn't believe in his own mother's integrity.

"One of us will have to accompany you inside the room," one of the guards said. It was the one who'd challenged him at the elevator a minute ago.

"That's fine," Vanessa said like it was her say. It wasn't. Nick could tell she'd been bluffing back there in the way her voice changed, moving up an octave. She spoke with more authority and straightened her back, standing tall at her full height of five-feet-seven-inches.

Nick pulled in a breath before taking the couple of steps inside the room. There were two beds; only one was occupied. His mother's was near the window. The blinds were closed, plunging the room into darkness. His eyes had a difficult time adjusting from the bright fluorescent lighting in the hallway to the wall sconce on what had to be the lowest dimmer setting.

One of the guards stepped in behind Nick, leaned his back against the door, and rested his right hand on the butt of his service weapon. Was it meant to remind Nick the guy would have the upper hand, so no funny business? This was Nick's mother's room. What the hell did the guard think Nick was going to do?

Vanessa slipped her hand in his as they both walked toward the bed. Normally, he would pull away from contact but not this time. Not while he walked up to the bed where his mother was either faking it or seriously injured. Either would gut him.

Beep. Beep. Beep.

Machines were hooked up to his sleeping mother. There

was white gauze wrapped around her head, covering her forehead.

Nick bit back a curse as he got close enough to see swollen eyes and a busted lip. She had five or six stitches holding her nose together. White hot rage caused his grip to tighten around Vanessa's hand. Rather than squeeze to the point of hurting her, he let go.

"I'll make sure this doesn't happen again, Nick," she whispered as his mother's eyes fluttered open. "I'll make sure she's safe from here on out."

There was a hint of grandeur in Vanessa's voice along with a whole heap of sympathy. It dawned on him why. She would be able to get his mother's trial moved away from Lone Star Pass now. This had to be the proof she'd been looking for.

Guilt slammed into him for doubting his mother. It struck him as odd that she could be downright evil on the one hand and a victim on the other. He didn't have it inside him to hate her as he saw her try to smile at him. She winced in pain, so he reached out to touch her hand, and then realized her wrists were cuffed to the bed. It shouldn't shock or anger him, but it did.

What if there was a fire?

Okay, he could admit the thought was a little out there. She had guards stationed twenty-four hours a day as far as he could tell. The men had been pushy with his mother's attorney. It wouldn't look good for a prisoner to die on their watch. The media would have a field day. They would ensure she made it out alive, if only to save their own hides.

His mother's face twisted in pain. She tried to speak.

Nick moved close to her ear and whispered, "It's okay. I'm here. Don't hurt yourself."

As much as he wanted to hear what she wanted to say,

there would be time later. Looking at her as she lay helpless, bound to a hospital bed, all his anger toward her subsided. For now.

She squeezed his hand.

"I'm going to make certain you are never back in that jail cell again," Vanessa promised, renewed anger and something that sounded a lot like resolve seethed in her tone. "This is totally unacceptable."

His mother squeezed again, and gave a little nod. She closed her eyes as though keeping them open required too much effort on her part.

"Rest," he said to her. The truth would come out soon enough. She might be in the wrong. Maybe she brought this on herself. Or maybe someone decided to meter out their own form of justice. His mother wasn't street-smart or tough. Brittle would be a better word to describe her. Lost would also fit. How on earth had she gone so far off the rails? He would blame it on her drinking problem, except there were plenty of folks in the same situation who didn't plan and attempt to execute a murder plot.

What was so broken in her that caused her to decide that *that* might be a viable solution? Her money-grabbing tendencies had gone off the rails. So had her judgment.

Rather than churn those questions over and over again in his mind, he put them to bed. He might never know the real reasons she did what she'd done. It was something he was going to have to accept and live with for the rest of his life. The only real question in his mind was whether or not he could stand behind her during her trial. Looking at her now, all the rage had dissipated like storm clouds after a good rain and all he felt was sympathy.

Vanessa excused herself to make a call. She walked over toward the door, and then stepped inside the private bathroom. The door was left open enough for him to hear the hum of her voice. She spoke low enough that he couldn't make out the words. Once again, he wouldn't want to be on the other side of that conversation.

Nick pulled up a chair and sat with his mother. His thoughts bounced around as he watched her eyes flutter, trying to stay open but losing the battle. It was like watching a butterfly caught in the wind.

He fished out his cell phone and fired off an update to the group chat, letting everyone know their mother was alive and that he was with her because of Vanessa. He finished by saying he would give them the green light if and when she could accept other visitors.

The group chat started blowing up with messages of concern and gratitude. He and his brothers had been on the same page about their mother. It didn't look as though anything had changed.

His father, however, was maintaining silence. Vanessa had already mentioned the fact Keifer Firebrand was cutting his wife off financially. As much as Nick couldn't imagine the betrayal his father must have felt, must still feel, he couldn't fathom kicking someone when they were down. The vow his father had taken meant through thick and thin, as far as Nick was concerned. It was the only reason to pledge spending the rest of his life with someone. And since marriage was working out so well for his parents, he'd given up on the institution a long time ago.

The shooter from this morning kept nagging him. He'd been convinced the bullet was meant for him as some kind of revenge against his family. But Vanessa hadn't batted an eyelash at insisting she'd been the target. Why? What else was there to the story?

VANESSA WAS LIVID. It had been hours since the incident occurred at the jail and there was still no report available to her. She needed to know what ammunition she had to work with so she knew which way to go with her next steps. If the fight was blamed on Jackie Firebrand, there would be less sympathy.

She blew out a frustrated breath.

"Sergeant, put me through to Warden Dennison," Vanessa finally snapped. The sergeant's excuse of needing to have the proper signatures before he could turn over the incident report didn't hold water. He was holding something back, and she intended to find out what it was.

Of course, her first thought was that the jailors looked the other way because they didn't have a whole lot of sympathy for someone incarcerated for attempted murder. The jail population in a county like this one had its fair share of felons. She'd read the report to find out what kind of criminals her client was being housed with. In this area, there were more drug crimes based on remote drug labs being busted than murderers. Drugs were followed by domestic violence and theft. The fourth reason caused her stomach to twist into a knot because it involved sex workers. Young women, often runaways, found themselves caught up in human trafficking. It was rampant, and it didn't matter which city or county was involved.

The thought of all those young lives being damaged forever, even when they were recovered and offered treatment, made her sick. Those were the cases she refused to defend. In fact, her specialty was taking on cases where a defendant truly needed a good defense attorney. Before she'd taken over the helm of her father's firm, she'd turned away anyone she didn't truly believe in. Her father had given her carte blanch when it came to doing pro-bono work, and fighting against injustice. The luxury of cherry-picking cases diminished the minute she'd been handed the financial sheets. Now that she knew how deep her father's gambling problem had been, she wondered how much guilt played a role in how lenient he'd been with her after law school. Did allowing her to take on pro-bono work somehow absolve him from his sins? Because other than what he'd done to her mother, which had been awful, she'd believed the man walked on water.

Now that she was seeing his dark side, it was impossible to hold him in the same light. But then, didn't every daughter see what they wanted to in their father?

Despite not being able to afford to do pro-bono work any longer, Vanessa made an exception for Nick's mother. Jackie Firebrand had no financial means, which wasn't going to stop Vanessa from taking the case, no matter how much it might cost in the end. If she won, there would be a big payoff. Getting someone of her stature to change her plea, and then getting her off would be a huge career boost. If Vanessa lost, her solo career would be over before it got off the ground. As much as she didn't want to admit it to herself, the rumor going around that she'd been riding her father's coattails had bothered her.

This case could redeem her reputation. Nick, however, was convinced his mother was guilty. The Nick she'd known had been the definition of honor and pride—pride he was no doubt having to swallow now to be in this room. Visiting his mother was a huge step in the right direction. The mountain he had to climb to get over the past was almost the same size as the one Vanessa had to in order to win this case.

For the first time in her career, Vanessa worried she might not be up to the task at hand. Defending Jackie Firebrand had been a snap decision. An excuse to come back to Lone Star Pass?

"That won't be necessary, Ms. Mosely," the sergeant said after a long pause. She'd given him the space to think about the possible consequences of his actions, remaining silent while her mind worked overtime. The game, at that point, had become one of patience. Talking first was the equivalent of the staring game. The one who blinked first lost.

"Does that mean you're sending the report right now?" she said after issuing a sharp sigh.

A ding sounded, indicating her phone just received an e-mail.

"You should have it in your inbox," Sergeant Hopper said. "I apologize for the delay in sending the report." He paused. "You know how it is with all the red tape involved."

"Red tape?" she asked, but the question was rhetorical. "A court of law would see that as withholding valuable evidence. Not to mention slap you with an obstruction of justice charge." The warden was her uncle on her mother's side. Delbert Wayne. They weren't close but family bonds still meant something. It wasn't a card she'd intended to play but a phone call to her mother would have made a difference. In fact, Vanessa had been in town several days and had yet to reach out to her mother. Their relationship became strained the more it appeared that Vanessa was choosing her father over her mother. Vanessa listened to him, took his advice. She would go to her grave wondering why her parents ever got married in the first place when they appeared to hate each other. The term 'opposites attract' came to mind but didn't there have to be some common ground?

"Once again, Ms. Mosely, I apologize for the delay," Sergeant Hopper said. "Please let me know if I can be of further assistance."

She was pushing it with the threats, and he probably knew it too. "I'll be in touch."

After ending the call, she immediately pulled up the report and skimmed it before heading into the room where Nick sat at his mother's bedside. According to the report, Jackie slipped on a wet floor during kitchen duty and face-planted on the stove. Pictures were taken to back up the story but she would bet money this was like reading a fable, and not what really happened. It was also produced in a hurry. Therefore, mistakes could have been made. Mistakes she could use to shoot holes in the report and question its validity. Mistakes she could use in her argument the truth had been covered up to save the reputation of the jail. Mistakes she could use to add ammunition to her relocation request.

Where was the part about there being a disagreement over the meal at lunch? The sergeant had said he understood a group of women locked arms around fighting inmates, making it difficult for jailers to see let alone separate them.

Face and head lacerations. Those were real. Second-degree burns on her right side. If Mrs. Firebrand had face-planted against the stove, like the report said, where did the burns on her right hip come from?

Slipping on a wet floor was suspect, as well. Would someone be mopping while folks were in the kitchen cooking, as the report said Mrs. Firebrand had been doing? Vanessa had questions as to whether the floor was wet before the fall or if someone threw a bucket of water on it after. Neither explained two cracked ribs if she supposedly hit her head on the stove and again on the hard floor.

She realized she was white-knuckling her cell. Since her track record wasn't exactly stellar when it came to not breaking the screen, she intentionally loosened her grip. This report was signed off on by her uncle. His signature looked hastily scribbled on there. Someone might have been waiting to slip it inside a stack of papers so he would sign without really paying attention. People got used to things being handled a certain way. If this report was slipped in and no attention was called to it, she could see a scenario where her uncle would rubber stamp it in a manner of speaking.

For Mrs. Firebrand, Vanessa wanted justice. For Nick, Vanessa wanted justice. For all inmates who were unjustly treated, Vanessa wanted justice.

This seemed like a good time to remind herself this report would give her the ammunition to prove her client wasn't safe inside county lockup. Therefore, Mrs. Firebrand needed to be moved after release from the hospital. Should she give her uncle a heads-up as to what was coming? He, no doubt, would come under fire.

If this report saw the light of day outside of certain circles, his record and reputation would take a serious hit. Actions were like dominoes.

There was another, more immediate problem. What the hell was Nick going to do when he got hold of this information? She had to be honest with him, no matter how much it might pain her to do it. This news was going to rip his heart out. She couldn't afford for him to go off on a tangent either. Could he remain calm after reading the abuse his mother had endured?

Reading on, it was impossible for Mrs. Firebrand to

sustain the kinds of injuries she had in one fall even if she did also hit her head on the tile flooring. The busted nose that required stitches, along with more stitches on the crown of her head made no sense based on these findings. The doctor's report would prove to any reasonable person this report was pure fiction.

In her experience, guards wouldn't testify against each other. They lived by a code that said they watched each other's backs. Even a good guard would look the other way rather than turn on someone they worked with side-by-side in a jail. Because it would be too easy for other guards to 'accidently' leave them out on the yard alone with some of the more violent offenders. It might all read like a bad movie script, but it was real. It happened. Guards sometimes became sympathetic to inmates. There was an entirely different economy that ran in jails and prisons based on the firsthand accounts of some of her clients.

Vanessa reenacted the report, using the bathroom sink as 'the stove.'

It was almost insulting the sergeant would approve this account, let alone get her uncle to sign off. Did he think she was incompetent?

Taking in a deep breath, she headed into the next room to deliver the news.

6

The second Nick looked up and caught the expression on Vanessa's face, he knew bad news was coming. As she walked over to him and he got a closer look, he saw the seriousness of what she was about to say in her eyes before she opened her mouth to speak.

"Who was on the phone?" he asked in a low voice so as not to disturb his mother any more than necessary.

"The sergeant."

"I'm guessing he delivered the report," he continued.

"You're not going to like it," she said. He noticed she was white-knuckling her phone. More bad signs.

"Let's see it," he said, grinding his back teeth, which indicated his stress meter was flying off the charts.

"Before I show you this, keep in mind that whatever you do next could mean the difference between you being locked up and your freedom," Vanessa pointed out. The fact she felt the need to say something like that to him said he was about to get mad, like Bruce Banner turning into the Hulk type furious.

"What exactly is in that report?" he asked.

"It's hard to read, Nick. I'm not going to lie about that," she said, locking gazes. The familiar jolt of electricity shot through him. It didn't matter if it was physical touch or gazes touching, the effect was the same and not something he wanted to think too hard about.

"I'm looking at the result," he said, motioning toward his sleeping mother. Every few minutes, her eyes blinked open or she squeezed his hand. "Reading the report couldn't possibly fire me up any more than I already am."

She cocked an eyebrow. "You're saying that because you haven't read this yet."

There was probably a lot of truth to the statement. He'd had to restrain himself from putting his fist through the wall as it was after seeing his mother's injuries for himself. But this would possibly start them on a trail that might lead them to the shooter. Or was it the other way around? Was the beat down, and that was the only way to describe what happened to his mother, to bring him out into the open? Or Vanessa? She'd been confident the shooter was after her. Was that the default logic for someone in her line of work?

Not many folks wanted to take down ranchers by nature of their job. In fact, most ranching communities were tight-knit and helped each other out. Of course, there were poachers who hunted on ranch land or stole cattle. By and large, ranching was a peaceful job.

"I do this for a living, and it was a lot for me," she continued. "Just remember this report is useful in that I can get the trial moved away from this area where your mother won't get a fair trial. And, more importantly, I can use it to have her moved somewhere safe until her court date."

"And then what?" he asked in a whisper. If his mother heard this conversation and understood the implications from it, would she become depressed? Take her own life?

There was a time when these questions wouldn't have crossed his mind. But there he was, asking.

"It'll be me doing my job," she said with defensiveness in her tone.

"I'm sure the news coverage won't hurt your career once word leaks out," he quipped.

The hurt look on her face had him wishing he could take those words back almost immediately.

"Is that what you think of me, Nick?" She set the phone down on the bed, then tapped the screen.

"No, of course not," he said, not afraid to beg her forgiveness at this point. His anger was talking but he didn't have a right to take it out on her.

"Here you go. Read on," she said. With that, she walked out of the room. The fact she turned her head toward the opposite wall had him thinking she was covering her tears. The sniffle as she exited the room confirmed his suspicion.

Damn. He was a jerk.

Nick needed to apologize. Right now, though, the need to read the report and stay by his mother's side won. Vanessa wouldn't want him coming after her anyway. That had never been her style. When she needed a minute, she *needed* a minute. She would come back when she was ready to talk. And he would say whatever it took in order to get her to forgive him.

The words on the screen amped up his anger by leaps. The report—if it could be called that—was a joke. Vanessa had been right. His teapot was boiling over. The whistle was sounding. It was taking every ounce of willpower to stay right where he was and not storm the county jail demanding justice. This was criminal. The fact guards had looked the other way and allowed this to happen on their watch was unthinkable.

There was no explanation of how the beating started. Only the water excuse. She would have had to take one helluva fall in close quarters to do the amount of damage she'd endured. Being locked inside a giant pinball machine would be a better way to explain what had happened to her.

This was disgusting. It was wrong on so many levels. Granted, his mother was in jail. She'd committed a crime and justice needed to be metered out and served. She had to pay for what she'd done. Almost done.

It was lucky for her that she hadn't been able to go through with her plan or she would be facing an even worse sentence. And even if his mother had said something stupid in jail, she didn't deserve this kind of beatdown. Take away her dinner or make her clean the floors with a toothbrush. Don't turn your back and allow other inmates to treat her like a punching bag.

This was unacceptable.

Nick's thoughts shifted to Vanessa because if he focused on the report much longer, he wasn't sure he could stop himself from doing something he would live to regret. He thought about how Vanessa had tried to prepare him for what he was about to read. She'd done her best to talk him off a ledge he'd had yet to get on.

Snapping at her was a jerk move. He'd been unfair to her and downright rude. Vanessa was genuinely trying to help his mother. Being on her side would help him stay in the loop of his mother's chances and her trial, so he vowed to keep his sarcasm to himself. Vanessa had a way of pushing his buttons like no one else had ever been able to do. His heart wanted to argue there was another reason she was the only one who could strike him at the core. Whatever they had was a long time ago. Now? All he felt was residual, unresolved feelings lingering. A blast from the past.

A good dose of reality was all he needed to keep him in check. Because he'd thought about kissing her more than he should. And he refused to go there, where Vanessa had been his one true love. They'd been kids. Of course, what they'd shared had felt special. Hormones heightened everything, which explained why he'd never reached those heights with anyone since. It wasn't true love. It was impaired memory.

Vanessa returned with a fierce expression that almost dared him to speak. She planted a fisted hand on her right hip. "Well."

"I apologize for what I said a few minutes ago," he began, doing his best to keep his anger over the situation in check without lashing out at someone who didn't deserve it. After all, making her feel bad was misdirected and not his intention. "This should help you file everything you need to get her to a safe place."

She nodded as she looked at him.

"Hey, I couldn't feel worse for my actions," he continued.

She dismissed him with a look. "We don't have time."

With that, she held her hand out flat and took a step toward him. Her puffy eyes said she'd been crying. He felt like a real jerk.

"It's your word against Hopper's but a fight is consistent with her injuries," she finally said.

Nick placed the phone on her palm. His fingers grazed her skin, and the explosion at contact caught him off guard. He cleared his throat to ease some of the sudden dryness and tried to catch her gaze to see if her reaction was the same. She refused to look at him.

The rejection was fair but he hated it.

LOOKING into Nick's eyes right now would be like staring at an eclipse. It might be beautiful for a few seconds, but it would burn her eyes in the long run, causing permanent damage.

"The hospital is short staffed, so the doctor is tied up," she informed. "A nurse filled me in and gave me access to the chart. As you can already see, the injuries are bad. I need my phone so I can take a picture of the file before she realizes she just violated HIPPA laws by giving me access in the first place."

"You'd find a way to finesse it out of her anyway," he said with a half-smile.

She clamped her mouth shut because it wanted to tell him it was too late for compliments. He'd been clear about what he thought about her. They didn't need to engage in a seesaw of emotions for her to realize he would never forgive the past. There wasn't anything she could do about it. Finding a solid defense for his mother was repayment enough for the guilty conscience she'd been carrying around all these years. Breaking his heart had gutted her.

Vanessa stopped right there. The realization she'd taken the case as some sort of atonement to Nick shocked her, but this wasn't the time to analyze their non-relationship. Not when she had a case to win.

She excused herself and snapped the pictures needed as she built her case. Next, she needed to file a motion to change venue for the trial using the evidence she'd collected so far. The shooter from this morning would help in her claim no one connected to the case was safe anywhere near Lone Star Pass. Her body involuntarily shivered at the reality of almost being shot today. And then there was all

NICK: Firebrand Cowboys 61

the conflicting emotions about her father on top of everything else. The pain of losing him was still raw. The sense of loss that came with finding out that he wasn't who she'd believed him to be was still raw. The guilt that came with being angry at someone who was gone was still raw.

"Ma'am, you'll have to get what you need and leave," the guard from earlier said. "I got a call from my commanding officer."

"Okay," she said, unsure of how she would get Nick to leave his mother's side.

She thanked the nurse before returning to the room to find Nick with his head bowed on clasped hands. The image sent a shot straight to her heart. A strong person like him would feel completely helpless in this situation, and it would hit him where it hurt.

The image gave her even more resolve to protect the woman in the hospital bed, machines beeping, reminding Vanessa how fragile life could be.

"I need to get over to the courts to file a few motions to get your mother to safety," she said to Nick, hating to interrupt him.

"I'm going with you," he said, immediately standing. "After what happened this morning, I don't want you to be alone."

"You're my ride," she pointed out.

"Right," he said. "That too."

The tender expression on his face when he looked down at his mother brought more tears to Vanessa's eyes. She was not a crier.

"I'll be back as soon as I can," he said in almost a whisper. "And, Mom, I want you to hang on. Fight. Okay? You got this. You can do this."

The moment was so special and personal Vanessa

turned around to give him privacy. She stared at the wall, trying not to let the floodgates open. Losing her father so recently made this hit her in a different light. With cases on hold and the firm in trouble, she hadn't given herself much more than two seconds to grieve. If she lost the business, she would lose his legacy. It was all she had left of him and the plans they'd made. His legacy to her might be complicated but that didn't stop her from loving him.

She'd been practicing law more than a decade and still hadn't made her mark. Instead, she'd focused on taking cases she cared about, rather than prioritizing lucrative ones. Her father, on the other hand, could have put the Lincoln lawyer to shame. The man had envelopes stuffed with cash strategically hidden in his office. Of course, the money was kept off the books and much of it was most likely gambled away. For the life of her, she couldn't find enough lying around to make a difference in balancing the books.

"Ready?" Nick finally asked as he crossed the room.

She nodded before walking out to the truck together, climbing inside, and then hitting the road.

Vanessa dismissed the thought a bookie could have been responsible for the warning shot this morning. She knew enough about guns to realize how difficult the shot would have been at a distance on a windy day. She'd had to defend folks using wind velocity to prove they couldn't have been responsible for hitting a target.

It was starting to sink in with her that *she* had been someone's target practice a few hours ago. The reality was shocking and sobering all at once.

Was the incident related to this case? Or was it a threat? A way to show that the shooter could get her if he or she wanted to? Point out the fact she was alive because they'd allowed her to live?

That was a scary thought. A little too real.

All she had to do was read through her e-mails to drum up half a dozen names of people who could be placed on a suspect list. If she so much as didn't look at a client right, they got nervous. Especially the cases she'd picked up from her father. He was less discretionary when it came to the kinds of clients he took on. There were cases she knew better than to ask about with clients who only showed up to the office after the building had been cleared. What had her father gotten himself into? Or was she jumping the gun? Letting her imagination run wild?

The short answer was probably a resounding *yes*.

Another realistic possibility for this morning's shooter was because of this case. Jackie Firebrand wasn't the warm and fuzzy type, and her reputation wasn't exactly stellar. She wasn't as popular in town as her sister-in-law. Who didn't love Lucia Firebrand? Vanessa didn't know her very well and she loved her based on the interactions they'd had. Lucia was the type to welcome anyone and everyone with open arms. Jackie was stiffer and far more closed off.

There had to be a good reason for Jackie's demeanor. People weren't generally born bad. They were neglected and left to their own devices. They were treated like they weren't important. They were emotionally abused. They were physically abused.

Was Vanessa onto something here with her brainstorming? Mrs. Firebrand wouldn't be up to speaking for days, maybe longer. Vanessa would have to arrange for a laptop or iPad with a writing utensil to be brought into the room for her client to be able to communicate more comfortably or at all.

"You've been quiet on the ride over," Nick said, interrupting her train of thought.

"I'm thinking."

"I can tell," he said. "Did you solve world peace?"

The light-hearted comment caught her off guard. She smiled despite herself.

"Almost," she said. "Did you know that it takes an average of seventeen minutes to regain concentration on a task once it's been broken?"

"I did not," he quipped. And then his serious demeanor returned. "I haven't thanked you for what you're doing for my mother."

"It's my job," she said.

He gave a slight nod as he pulled into the courthouse parking lot. "Can I ask a question that's been bugging me all day?"

"Go ahead."

Nick claimed a parking spot and then cut off the engine. "Why were you so certain the shooter was after you?"

Did she want to answer that? Did she want to go into the shady clients her father worked with? Or the gambling debts? Nick already disliked her father. Did she want to make it worse? Then again, was it right to withhold information from him when his life could be at risk?

7

Nick waited for Vanessa's response.

"I can't think of a reason anyone would try to shoot at you," she finally said. "I chose myself by default."

The answer she gave took too long to get there. The way she'd responded in the moment when it had happened spoke volumes. She'd instantly dismissed the notion that the shooter could be aiming for anyone else but her. There was a story behind her response that he intended to find.

Before he could say anything else, she was reaching for the door handle. He settled into his seat and fished out his phone.

"Are you coming?" she asked when he didn't make a move for the door.

"I figure you'll be safe inside a courthouse," he said. "Plus, you don't need me to tell you how to do your job at this point. I'll be right here waiting when you're finished."

"Alright," she said with a determined set to her chin. She exited and made a beeline straight for the courthouse. He scanned the area for any signs of danger and then didn't take his eyes off her until she made it safely inside. She was holding back, keeping something from him. Why?

While Vanessa did her thing, Nick figured this would be a good time to make a few phone calls. Besides, it wasn't like he could ask her any more questions. His first call was to his twin. Then, he called his brother Kellan who was the oldest.

"Where the hell is our father?" he asked after perfunctory greetings.

"That's a good question," Kellan said. "I imagine he's out working cattle, now that Uncle Brodie has had to take a step back after his stroke."

"Shouldn't he be at the hospital with his wife?" Nick asked, not masking the bitterness to his tone.

Kellan's lack of immediate response said it was a rare time his brother didn't know how to respond. He cleared his throat. "How is she?"

"Not good," Nick said. "But she'll live."

"How bad is it?" Kellan's voice dropped an octave as concern wound its way in.

"Cracked ribs, burns on her body, and her face looks like she spent five rounds in a street fight with a professional MMA fighter," Nick ground out.

"Damn," was all Kellan said. "Did she start it?"

"Even if she did, she didn't deserve to be beaten up like this," he defended.

"Doesn't something like this have to be documented?" Kellan asked.

"The report is trash," Nick stated. "There's no way our mother could have sustained this level of injury based on slipping on a wet floor."

"Can she tell her side of it, or..." Kellan didn't—couldn't?—finish the sentence. The catch in his throat said his emotions were getting the best of him.

"The good news here is that she's in the hospital, being guarded, and is on the road to healing," Nick informed. "Believe it or not, it could have been worse."

"For her to be this bad off, guards had to have looked the other way once," Kellan surmised.

"That's my impression too," Nick confirmed. "But they won't now because eyes are on them."

"How do we get her out of there?" Kellan continued.

"Vanessa is working on it," Nick said.

"Mosely?"

"Yes," Nick confirmed.

"I heard her father passed away," Kellan said.

Why did his brother know that? Then again, Kellan always cared about what was happening around them. Was it because he was the oldest? He felt responsible for everyone? He could be a jerk, but he'd always looked out for the family, doing what he believed was in their best interest. It didn't mean he was always right. And he had a stubborn streak a mile long. But that was Kellan. His divorce had ramped up his anger several notches. To his credit, though, he didn't appear to hold a grudge against Liv after she divorced him to marry their cousin Corbin. Then again, Liv and Corbin had grown up best friends. Everyone but Kellan saw the two should have married a long time ago.

Life was funny that way. There were so many twists and turns that it was hard not to be thrown off track. Stay the course long enough, though, and things had a way of righting themselves eventually.

"That's right," Nick said, rejoining the conversation. "Why do you know this?"

"I keep my ear to the ground," Kellan said. Just as Nick thought. His brother paid attention to everything going on, whereas Nick kept to himself more and more. Was that the reason his once-lively dating life had shriveled up like a prune? To be fair, he'd always believed in monogamy. Just not the forever kind of commitment.

"Someone shot at us this morning," Nick said on sharp sigh.

"What the hell?"

"I know," Nick said. What the hell indeed. "Vanessa is convinced she was the target but I'm not so certain after everything that's been going on with the family. Our mother was too out of it and in pain to speak."

"Meaning? She couldn't have been the one to order a hit," Kellan said. "And she wouldn't on her own son or the person trying to get her out of a conviction."

Sadly, there were scenarios Nick could think that would make something bad happening to Vanessa worth it for his mother. For instance, it would be impossible to go to trial if her attorney was dead. The shooter had missed by a decent margin. The distance and wind could have been responsible. In fact, they were likely the culprits. A sharpshooter would take those factors into account, make adjustments. Come to think of it, the shooter had only fired once. Granted, Nick had dived on top of Vanessa to protect her. But a committed shooter wouldn't let that stand in his way. The jail cops had run out so fast that Nick hadn't had time to look around for shell casings to get a sense of what kind of rifle had been used. There would be a ballistics report somewhere. Could Vanessa subpoena the report? Based on the mistakes in the last one she'd requested, he doubted it would matter. Anyway, he digressed.

"I don't think she would order a hit on her attorney," Nick finally said to his brother.

"If the guards didn't protect our mother, she either upset

them in some way or they turned their back on her because they don't care what happens to her," Kellan pointed out.

"My thoughts exactly."

And yet, something wasn't adding up.

"Why take the hit on their record, though?" he asked Kellan, thinking out loud. "Aren't jails rated on those factors?"

"Could be the main reason they went with the whole 'slipped on a wet floor' excuse," Kellan pointed out.

"If the official record reflected an accident, they wouldn't be in hot water," Nick deduced.

"And if no one was there to contest the report, the world wouldn't be the wiser," Kellan said.

Again, guilt slammed into Nick for not visiting his mother sooner. "I can't help but think this wouldn't have happened if I'd shown up. The guards must know she never gets visitors."

"Don't do that to yourself, Nick."

"What?" he asked. "Take responsibility?"

"Don't blame yourself for something none of us did," Kellan said. "Not even our father stopped by to visit his wife."

Of course, it looked like no one cared what happened to her. The bastards believed they could get away with anything they wanted and no one would be the wiser. Would an off-duty guard go out of his way to shoot at a visitor? Someone who could protest?

No, this trail didn't jive. Every inmate had an attorney, court-appointed or otherwise. Any lawyer worth his or her salt would put a stop to their client being manhandled. Then again, an overworked public defender might look the other way or be so overloaded with work that they made mistakes.

Nick wondered how often that happened. It had to be more than he realized. Then again, he had very little experience dealing with jails and criminals other than poachers. His role with those bastards was to track them and then call the law.

"Nick?"

Kellan's voice shook him out of his revelry.

"I know," Nick responded. "No blaming myself for something outside of my control."

He heard himself say the words. Acting on them was a whole different ballgame.

"Should we station someone at the hospital?" Kellan asked.

"It's not a bad idea," Nick admitted. "The only reason I was allowed in the room was because of Vanessa. Without her, I'm afraid it'll be folks waiting in the lobby."

"I'll set up shifts," Kellan said.

"What about Rowan?" Nick asked, figuring if anyone knew his whereabouts it would be Kellan.

"No idea, man," Kellan said, sounding defeated. "He didn't say much about where he was going, for how long, or when he'd be back if he decides to come home again."

"Is not coming back a possibility?" Nick asked, more than surprised his brother would up and leave forever without explaining himself further. Then again, nothing should shock him lately.

"You got me," Kellan said. "Wouldn't rule it out, though."

Nick blew out a breath. "I guess the whole family dynamic is changing. Folks are pairing up, becoming families, getting married."

Kellan was quiet after the last word was spoken. Damn. Nick realized his brother's divorce had to still sting. He wasn't trying to poke at a sore spot.

"Then there's Uncle Brodie's stroke and the reallocation of inheritance and work," Nick continued, hoping to get the conversation back on track.

"It's been a lot," Kellan said after clearing his throat. "Not to mention the situation with our mother." A pause came before, "Hold on. I think I see our father." Another pause. "Yes, that's him. I better go catch him up to date."

"Maybe he can take the first shift," Nick said sarcastically. The man abandoned his wife. No matter how much Keifer Firebrand claimed to have changed, he was still cut from the same cloth.

"We'll see," Kellan said with little hope in his voice.

"Watch your back, okay?" Nick felt the need to add.

"You too," Kellan said. "We need you around here."

The two exchanged goodbyes around the same moment Vanessa exited the building. One look at her face said she was frustrated or worried, or both. A sinking feeling took hold. Should Nick be worried about her expression?

~

"WHAT HAPPENED?" Nick asked, his question was fair.

"Nothing," Vanessa said on a frustrated sigh. "The judge is out playing golf."

"Should we make a trip to the public course?" Nick asked.

"He's at Pebble Beach," she said, pinching the bridge of her nose. "Won't be back on the bench until tomorrow afternoon."

It occurred to her the day was getting away from her and she hadn't eaten in more hours than she cared to count.

Nick started the engine. "You have a headache?"

"It's from hunger," she admitted. "But I'm fine. There's a lot to think through and a whole lot to do."

"We'll get food first," he said, starting the engine. "No one can think straight when they're starved, especially not you. Remember the chem test you failed because you forgot to eat lunch and tried to power through the test anyway?"

"I failed because I studied for the wrong test," she defended with a small smile.

"Are you kidding me?" he quipped. "You knew chem like the back of your hand. All you would have needed was a quick review, but you were hungry, so you weren't thinking straight. Then, you blanked out in chem."

"I got lucky that my teacher let me retake the test," she said. "Those testing center teachers weren't always so nice."

"You did alright for yourself," he said, which filled her with a sense of pride.

"I was practicing the kind of law that I wanted to before my father..." She had to stop for a minute so she could collect herself. "You know...passed."

"I'm sorry about losing your father, Vanessa. I really am," Nick said in a voice that almost had her believing he meant it. How could he? The two had been gasoline on fire. Although, to be fair, her father was most of the blaze. Nick was respectful. He had honor. He could get along with anyone if he put his mind to it. Her father had believed a relationship in a small town like Lone Star Pass would somehow corrupt her into wanting to give up on her dreams of becoming a lawyer.

Her father didn't have the first idea of how supportive Nick had always been. Wouldn't listen to reason either. He was convinced Nick would hold her back in the end. Of course, that wasn't how he put it back in high school. He had to know she would have rebelled against the idea. No.

Her father was smarter than that, and she respected him too much to go against his wishes for her.

Looking back, she couldn't believe she'd been such a pushover. Then again, she'd loved her father and believed he wanted the best for her. The man had her convinced of it anyway. Vanessa had bought into his victim routine when it came to his relationship with her mother. He'd convinced Vanessa that her mother was the bad guy. He definitely brought out the worst in her mother. There'd be no argument coming from her there. It wasn't until Vanessa was much older that she realized her mother never said a mean-spirited word about her father behind his back. At least, not to Vanessa. Not to mention the fact her mother had always had to be the serious parent since her father had apparently threatened to take her to court to get full custody if she didn't comply with his requests. He was good at twisting words to benefit himself.

And wasn't she just like him? Or at the very least dyed from the same cloth?

It made her wonder if this was the reason her past relationships hadn't amounted to much. She'd convinced herself that she was too busy to put the time in. Looking back, she couldn't help but wonder if that was true.

Hunger was making her think too much about the past. Keep looking in the rearview and her future would smack her in the back of the head.

Plus, this was probably her brain's way of distracting her from the fact she'd been shot at today.

Vanessa bit back a yawn.

"You're hungry and tired," Nick said. "Not a good combination."

"Nothing I haven't dealt with before," she said.

"It's a good thing we're heading back to the ranch," he said. "Unless you want to pick up fast food along the way."

"How long until we reach your place?" she asked. The last thing she wanted was fried food.

"Another half an hour," he said after glancing at the clock. "Can you make it that long?"

"Sure," she said. "If you don't mind, I might lean my seat back and close my eyes."

"Go for it," he said, reaching for the CD player. He tapped a button, then the cab filled with soft jazz music. Her favorite artist. She must have given him a look because he said, "What? I like jazz every once in a while. You turned me onto it."

"I can't argue your taste," she said with a small smile. And then she closed her eyes and fell into a deep sleep.

8

When it came to Vanessa's sleeping habits, not much had changed. She'd passed out inside his truck, and didn't so much as blink while he carried her into the home he'd had built near Whispering Rock Lake.

This took him back to the weekends she'd slept this hard after a study binge. There was no waking her no matter how much he didn't want her to go hungry. So, he'd always buy a box of donuts to leave in her room for when she woke up starving, searching for anything to fill the emptiness in her stomach. Glazed had been her favorite. She would text the silliest pictures that also managed to be damned adorable. His teenage heart had fallen hook, line, and sinker for her.

Taking her into his guest room, he managed to peel back the covers without disturbing her. Next, he slid her shoes off. They had a small heel that could be used as a weapon if need be. He set those next to the nightstand so she could easily find them if she woke scared out of her mind in the unfamiliar place.

After pulling the covers over her, he retrieved her

handbag and laptop bag from his truck. She didn't travel light. In fact, he could use them for weight training or weapons if need be. No wonder her arms had muscle definition. Must be from packing these around all day.

Nick glanced around the area, remembering how easy it had been for others to trespass onto Firebrand property. The truth was that fencing was for the herd, not stalkers or murderers. Having a fence around the area in which cattle could graze freely kept them from wandering into creeks, where they got stuck and sometimes met their demise. Others broke bones trying to get out of the mud.

Until recently, he'd never considered someone trespassing to do members of the family harm. Which reminded him, he needed to send out a group text that he couldn't make a meeting happen tonight.

Once back inside, he sent the message, requesting to postpone until tomorrow at lunch. He had no idea how long Vanessa might sleep and he didn't want to wake her unnecessarily. His mother was safe in the hospital now that a family member would be on rotation. Based on the group chat, it had been decided updates would be posted each shift. Every person, save for Rowan, signed up to work a two-hour shift. At least their brother knew what was going on if he was in cell range. He was the only one not responding to the group chat. Then again, he'd needed a break. Nick wouldn't put it past Rowan to mute the group.

With everyone moving in different directions, it might be easier to have a Zoom meeting rather than trying to organize an in-person one.

Nick moved to the fridge, then located a container of his aunt's famous meatballs. He took out enough of a portion to fill his plate, and then nuked the meal. The smell alone was enough to make his mouth water. Speaking of which, his mouth was dry as the soil. He needed to drink water.

Seeing food also made him realize how hungry he was. He ate at the table, his phone sitting on top in case anyone needed to reach him.

As much as he wanted to feed Vanessa, he didn't want to wake her. The headaches she'd gotten when they were young had been no joke. She'd have to place cold, wet rags on her forehead and over her eyes while she slept in a room with black-out curtains. There was a special term if he remembered correctly. What was it? He snapped his finger as the answer came to him. Cluster migraines.

He didn't wish them on his worst enemy.

After eating and cleaning up, Nick headed to the shower. It was dark outside and they were in for the night. Even if Vanessa stirred, there wasn't much else they could do tonight. Ranch work started at five o'clock sharp. Most everyone would be asleep soon enough.

Nick realized he hadn't signed up for a slot at the hospital. Rather than stir up the group chat, he decided to shower and hit the hay.

Twenty minutes later, he was ready for bed. Before he slipped under the covers, he needed to check on Vanessa. The guest room was in the same hallway as the master, so it didn't take long before he stood at the door that was cracked. Vanessa had always been a heavy sleeper. There was comfort in knowing some things hadn't changed as he heard her softly snoring.

He grabbed a water bottle from the pantry before setting it on the nightstand in case she woke up thirsty. He didn't keep donuts in his pantry, so a banana would have to do the trick. Then, he got out of there so she didn't wake up to him in her room. The last thing he wanted to do was scare her when she was half awake.

Nick headed down the hall to his room.

A lot of good it did to go to bed. Sleep was about as close as August to snow-skiing weather. He turned onto his side and clamped his eyes shut. The shooter invaded his thoughts. Again, he wondered why Vanessa had been certain the shot had been meant for her.

Nick tossed and turned for a solid half hour before he gave up on getting sleep. He didn't want to chalk it up to the fact Vanessa Mosely was sleeping a few feet down the hallway in his guest bedroom, but she was even more beautiful than he remembered. Between her being here and visiting his mother, there was no way he was going to nod off.

He kicked off the covers and headed toward the kitchen. Halfway down the hall, he realized he had on boxers and nothing else. Doubling back, he tiptoed back to his room so as not to disturb her. The wood flooring in this house always creaked and groaned under his weight. He amused himself with the thought no one would ever be able to sneak up on him.

After sliding into a pair of jeans that he left unbuttoned at the waist, he headed back toward the kitchen. It was tempting to look in on Vanessa again, but he resisted. Instead, he kept his eyes forward until he reached the kitchen, where he put on a pot of coffee. Everyone had moved to those pods, it seemed, but he liked the way a pot smelled on the days he didn't work the ranch.

Nick couldn't remember the last day off he'd had. He'd been volunteering to cover for anyone and everyone in recent weeks. The smell of fresh brew perked up his mood considerably. He poured a cup and then sat down at the table with his phone. He researched Vanessa Mosely coupled with Mosely Law.

It took a while to scroll through all the entries but he finally found a blip of an article about her living off her father's reputation. Was that the real reason she'd taken the case? To prove herself?

There were other articles featuring her and a man-of-the-month on a date in a society page. There was no denying her beauty. Dressed up. Dressed down. Earlier in the morning when he'd been pressed on top of her, breathing in her scent, which was a mix of spring flowers and rain, his first thought was how beautiful she was. To be fair, that had been his second thought. His first was questioning how the hell he was going to get them out of the park alive.

Bullets had a way of taking center stage.

Vanessa had said she'd taken the case for his mother, insinuating it had also been because of him. Did it really have to do with proving herself? Taking on an unwinnable case to prove she had what it took?

He didn't want to doubt her intentions. And, honestly, he probably shouldn't even care as long as his mother received the best possible defense. Except that it did matter. To him. The reason Vanessa had taken on his mother's case was important.

He told himself that it was because she would cut bait if this went south. He tried to convince himself the reason he cared was for his mother and not some outdated sense of pride that had him wanting Vanessa to actually care.

Much more of this line of thinking and maybe he'd sign up for a poetry class so he could really wax poetic.

Who would want to hurt his mother in jail? Were they trying to silence her permanently? It occurred to Nick that

Vanessa could request to interview the former ranch hand that had been recruited by his mother in the murder plot, Decks, to see if he knew of others involved.

He made a mental note as he sipped his coffee. Dark roast was his favorite blend and he'd gotten the roast just right this time. Taking the time to watch the sunrise kept him going during difficult times—and his family had had their fair share.

A minute into his thoughts, he heard the shower turn on in the guest bathroom. Vanessa was awake. Should he confront her?

~

A QUICK SHOWER brought Vanessa back to life. During the last minute, she turned the water as cold as she could stand it. That always did the trick when she'd been up for two nights studying during law school finals or preparing for mock trial. There was no greater shock to the system than freezing cold water coming out of the faucet.

Looking back, she didn't have any carefree happy memories after leaving Lone Star Pass for Houston or even after in Austin. Of course, Nick might argue she didn't have a whole lot before leaving either, considering she'd stay in when everyone else was out having parties near the lake or driving to Austin for the weekend.

Living in Texas and never attending one Friday Night Lights game was probably considered a sin in most people's book. Throw her out of the state if needed, but she'd never been football obsessed. She'd never wanted to be a cheerleader on the sidelines of the sport Texans saw almost as a religion. And she sure as hell never wanted to date the quarterback. Not the running back. Not the defensive linemen...

Ranchers were more her style. One, in particular had caught her attention. Nick. She remembered to this day the first time she saw him. She'd been sitting on the side of the pool at his high school the day he first approached her. She must have been the sight. Her goggles were sitting on her forehead, hair tucked into her rubber swim cap. Top it all off with a very unattractive one-piece swimsuit. To this day, she had no idea what he'd seen in her. Nick was tall even back then. He had more muscles than most despite still needing to fill out his frame.

He'd sat down beside her and asked her name. They talked for a solid hour before being kicked out of the pool area so the coach could close up. He'd asked her out but she'd said no. To this day, she was still trying to figure out the reason for the rejection. If she had to guess, she'd say that in an instant, she'd known this guy was different and that he had the power to make her want to change her plans.

Vanessa sighed. Nick had been the one person she could see building a different life with and it had scared her to the core.

But that was a long time ago.

She refocused, and realized she didn't want to put her dirty clothes back on. So, she rummaged around in the bathroom to find something to wear. A clean-smelling bathrobe hung on the hook on back of the door, so she put the white cotton robe on and then hung up her towel so it could dry.

The robe fit a little too well. Did she want to know who it belonged to? Vanessa hadn't asked if Nick was married or seeing someone. A gorgeous, intelligent man like him could have his pick.

It had always been that way. Again, she wondered why

he'd chosen her. She'd been a little obnoxious with her know-it-all attitude. She could only hope time and maturity had tempered that trait.

Now, of course, she had to be right and maybe the smartest person in the room in order to mount a proper defense or innocent people went to jail. There was nothing smug about that. Life had very real consequences if she wasn't on her game. Which brought her to Jackie Firebrand.

A clank in the kitchen reminded her that Nick was awake. She had no idea what he was doing up at this hour. Did the man ever sleep?

It wasn't calving season when no one on the ranch got proper rest. Nick had admitted to falling asleep in class more than once and being jarred out of sleep by a ruler being smacked on top of his desk.

In a ranching community like Lone Star Pass, it wasn't uncommon for everyone to pitch in during calving season. Or so she'd been told. Vanessa never set foot in high school, except to use the pool so she could get into a good college.

Everything in her life had been geared toward graduating early, finishing college early, and then getting into a good law school early so she could hurry and get her degree. About halfway through all the rushing, she started wondering what all the hurrying had been about.

Because once she graduated, she'd been required to intern at her father's law office. Her workload had been twice that of everyone else's because she'd had to prove herself. Looking back, her father had been hard on her. He'd demanded a lot.

And for what?

She hardly saw him outside of the firm. Mainly because he worked all the time. When he wasn't working, he was gambling. Except she didn't know that until recently. He'd kept it hidden from her, making her wonder what else he'd kept from her.

With all the lies and cover-ups, she should probably hate her father. Or resent him at the very least. He would deserve it. Except she couldn't. Maybe it was the father-daughter bond or that she wanted to believe they had one.

Didn't people have to have open communication if they wanted to be able to trust each other? They certainly didn't hide their secrets or manipulate the people who loved them the most. They say love is blind. Vanessa was certain they were talking about romantic love. But the same applied to other relationships too. Like parental love, for instance. There, she'd been blind as a bat.

Working in law, she'd learned no one was all good or all bad. Her father had his good sides too. He loved her deeply. He wanted her to live with him. That wasn't always the case in divorces. He thought she hung the moon, though his need to protect her also made him controlling and overprotective. His personal drive was legendary, but he had flaws. Gambling, for one. Was it a coping mechanism for a stressful life? For defending criminals that he had to know were guilty. How many above-board people paid their lawyer with unmarked bills stuffed in an envelope?

When she asked her father about the payments, he shrugged and said some of his clients worked on a cash basis. Told her not to worry about it. Said not everyone had a bank account or trusted the system with their money. He said it didn't mean his clients were guilty of wrongdoing.

He also told her the easy answer was usually the right one. In the case of cash-filled envelopes, criminal was the easy answer.

Vanessa issued a sharp sigh. Since his death, she was

seeing just how complicated a man her father had been. But then, wasn't that always the case?

She couldn't count the number of times she'd been investigating a claim only to have her preconceived notion turned upside down. There was one time she was defending a mother who'd claimed an abusive husband. She was fighting for full custody of their eleven-year-old son, and Vanessa had taken the case pro-bono because the mother had no money. She worked a server job and had a side hustle selling thrift store items she bought and embellished. The second business helped make ends meet. The father had a history of blackout drinking but his friends swore on the Bible that he'd never been a mean drunk. Except his wife and son had unexplained bruises. The deeper Vanessa dug into the case against the husband, the less she liked him. He didn't come off as violent but he was lazy. He wasn't stepping up to do his part around the house despite his wife's two jobs. He worked part-time taking care of grass at the country club's golf course. His wife claimed he had a wandering eye.

And then the little boy slipped up. Said his mother accidentally dropped the iron on his arm and that was the reason for one of his bruises. Vanessa took the boy aside and asked a few more questions. The more he talked, the bigger the holes in his story became. She questioned him as gently as she could while needling around for the truth. Then, he broke down and cried for an hour. The term 'ugly cry' applied here. After, he unburdened himself of his mother's plans to take them far away because her internet business was making a lot of money and she didn't want the dad to lay claim to any of the profits.

Talk about a turn-around story. The mother had been a

sympathetic character. She wore long sleeves in the summer and heavy makeup around her eyes that simulated bruising.

Right up until the kid started talking, Vanessa had been ready to unleash hell on the dad. Instead, she focused on ensuring the dad got half of the business and checked into rehab. Fast forward four years, the dad was sober and employed full-time. He never missed a child support payment or his visitation.

The case had made her believe anything was possible if someone was determined enough. It had also taught her guilty people could come off as innocent if they tried. Jackie Firebrand rolled over the minute she'd been caught. A practiced criminal would have pled the fifth and asked for a lawyer.

Mrs. Firebrand might not be innocent, but it was possible she would never have gone through with the plan to kill either.

9

———

"Why did you really take on my mother's case?" Nick asked Vanessa as she walked into the kitchen. He cleared the sudden dryness in his throat at seeing her in nothing but a bathrobe.

"Who does this belong to?" she asked, motioning toward the robe and ignoring his question.

"I asked first," he said, which sent him back to middle school. Was he going to pull her ponytail next? "Meaning, I'll answer when you do."

"I already told you," she said. "Your mother called my father's firm. I stepped in since he can't."

He stood up and moved to the coffee machine. "That's not an answer."

"It's the only one I have," she defended.

"How did my mother even know your father?" he asked.

"That's a good question," she said. "I assumed she made the connection because of us and the fact my mother still lives here."

Nick grabbed a plate and then moved to the fridge to portion out meatballs. "You're probably starving."

"I could eat."

At least she'd dropped her question. The truth was that he didn't know who the bathrobe belonged to. It had to have been someone from his past who'd decided to leave something behind. No one had ever asked for it back, so he washed it and hung it in the guest bath.

The key to making sure everyone was on the same page in a relationship was keeping separate spaces. Nick never slept over at anyone else's place, despite being monogamous. If a guest wanted to stay over, he had a room just for that purpose. It might seem a little cold but it kept both parties from blurring the lines, him included.

In fairness, he didn't want to get too comfortable because he'd seen too many folks stay in bad relationships just because it was easier. Neither moving on when they should because they had a joint bank account or one person gave up their home to move in with the other.

Clear lines had to be drawn or he risked getting attached. As long as the other person had no problem with the arrangement, he would stay faithful until they agreed otherwise.

He nuked a plate before setting it on the table across from where he'd been sitting. "Meatballs okay?"

"Are you kidding?" she quipped, taking the seat with wide eyes. Her tongue darted across her lips. "These aren't just any meatballs. I could identify Aunt Lucia's based on smell alone."

"Coffee?" he asked with a smile despite himself.

"Yes, please," she said. "I had the worst headache but your guest room worked magic."

"It was probably just the nap that helped," he said as he poured a cup. "Sugar and cream?"

"A little cream is all," she said. "I drink way too much coffee to keep adding sugar."

Nick fixed her cup, and then brought it over to her.

She picked up the mug and wrapped her hands around it. "The warmth feels so good on my palms."

When her plate was cleaned, Nick rinsed it off and then placed it in the dishwasher. "I don't know."

Her left eyebrow flew up. "What?"

"Who the robe belongs to," he said. "Most likely a former friend of mine."

"Oh," she said. "Okay. Thanks for letting me know."

"You're welcome."

"The reason is two-fold," Vanessa said, picking up the other conversation thread. She didn't need to explain further for him to know what she referred to. "Call it a bout of nostalgia, but I really wanted to help your mother out. She was never mean to me when I was over, which I always appreciated. The second is that I want to prove myself. This case is going to be difficult and a challenge like this one could change my career."

"Still trying to please your father?" he asked in a voice so low he didn't think she'd heard him. Until he glanced over and saw the look on her face.

"My father's dead. Remember?" she said. It wasn't the words that were daggers to his heart so much as the hurt in her voice when she said them. The broken look in her eyes wasn't helping.

Nick was being a jerk. "Hey, sorry. All that between us with your father is ancient history. There's no reason to drudge up the past."

"It's fine," she said. Those two words meant anything but in the context of a conversation like this one.

"I didn't mean to cause—"

"I'm fine," she interrupted.

"You're here to help and I shouldn't—"

"Everything is fine."

Nick didn't have to study her face to know the opposite was true. Hell, he didn't have to look at her at all.

So, he took in a slow, deep breath and restarted. "I'm a jerk." He held his hand up when she opened her mouth to speak. "Turns out, letting go of the past is easier said than done, but I want to because you're here in good faith to help someone who desperately needs you. And, in truth, I'm not the jerk that I'm coming across as. Can you forgive me?"

"Are you suggesting we start over? Forget the past?" she asked.

He shook his head. "Why would I want that? I had some of my best memories of high school because of you."

"I didn't even go to your high school," she said, her tone softening.

Instead of continuing down that particular path, he changed the topic. "Why do you believe there is a coverup of what really happened to my mother in the jail?"

"They don't want a lawsuit or the bad publicity," she said. "Full disclosure, my uncle on my mother's side is the warden. We're not close so I don't have any cards to play there if your mother is sent back."

"She won't be," he insisted. "She can't be. It would be inhuman."

"A judge who is out playing golf in the middle of the week might not care what we think," she said. "I've seen it before with small-town judges. They don't seem to think they should be held accountable for doing their job."

"Why is that?"

"They're elected," she said. "They don't tend to rock the

boat of their constituents. People snap judge situations and sometimes want the book thrown at innocent people."

"She's not innocent."

"You've said that already," she pointed out.

"I hate what happened to her in there," he said before grinding his back teeth. "She should be able to pay her debt to society without being sent to the hospital."

"Agreed," she said.

"Are you trying to have her acquitted?" he asked.

"I went into this thinking that was going to be the play," she admitted. "Right now, I'd be happy to have her relocated somewhere safe to serve her time. I'm going to try to get the lightest sentence possible. And you should know that I'm prepared to fight hard for her."

"Tell me about the warden," he said.

"My uncle?" she asked, but it was rhetorical. "I know he and my mother haven't spoken in years."

The admission brought up another question. "What about you and your mother? Did you two ever fix your relationship after you moved?"

"No," she said with a frown. "Not to this day."

"She still lives in Lone Star Pass, correct?"

"That's right," she said. "We check in every few weeks. Sometimes a month goes by."

"Do you mind if I ask why?" he asked. Nick, of all people, understood complicated parent-child relationships.

She shrugged. "I was busy when I first moved away. Then, I got busier. The longer we went without talking, the easier it became to avoid making the call in the first place."

He nodded.

"I never knew what to say to her about going to live with my father," she continued. "At first, I left because I felt sorry for him and, to be honest, because he pressured me to.

Later, I realized he was good at guilt trips and that was the reason I chose to go to him." She shook her head. "It's weird how deep a father-daughter bond goes."

"I wouldn't know about that," he said. Not with eight brothers and no sisters in the family. His mother and Aunt Lucia were the only females around the ranch on a permanent basis until recently.

Vanessa cocked her head to one side. "Do you ever think about having children?"

"No," he said emphatically. "Actually, correction, I think about what a bad idea it would be for me to have a child."

"Can I ask why?"

Did he really have to explain? "With parents like mine, I honestly can say having a family never appealed to me."

"You would make an amazing father," she countered, much to his surprise.

The only time he'd ever thought about a future with someone was with her. Look where that had gotten him. "No, thanks."

∼

"What about you?" Nick asked, and his question caught her off guard.

It probably shouldn't, given the conversation.

"My career has always come first and it probably always will," she said. Speaking of family, Vanessa should call her mother. She filed the thought away on her list of things to do when this case was over. "People rarely change."

Nick got a little too quiet at her remark.

"I should probably give my uncle a heads up that I filed several motions earlier," she said, pushing up to standing. "Thanks for the dinner. It was amazing."

He nodded but didn't say a word. Instead, he drained his coffee cup and stood.

As he walked toward the sink, she reached for his arm. He stopped but didn't make eye contact.

In college, she'd dated a guy who couldn't be bothered to call if he decided to break their plans to go out with his buddies. Don't even get her started on the boy she'd started hanging out with as a study partner. He'd been good-looking and smart. Their texts became flirty. Next thing she knew, they were spending more time together outside of the library than in. Sebastian had asked her to go with him and three other couples to Dallas for the weekend. The guys had pitched in and rented a party bus so no one had to drive. Since she liked the other couples, she'd agreed.

The weekend had turned into one of the worst weekends of her life. Not only did her date get so drunk off his gourd, but he also slept with one of his friend's dates. Sebastian claimed to have spent the night in the hotel lobby, which she'd later learned wasn't the case.

He'd apologized a dozen times by the time they made it back to Austin. She couldn't stand to sit next to him on the ride back. And she sure as hell couldn't find it in her heart to forgive him. The whole event was gross and she wanted nothing to do with him after. So, it was the worst when he ended up in two of her classes the next semester and, as her luck would have it, her litigation partner in a mock trial.

"I was a jerk all those years ago," she managed to drum up the courage to say. "Leaving the way I did was cruel and I would handle everything so differently now. Walking away from Lone Star Pass, from you, was the hardest thing I've ever done. I did it for all the wrong reasons."

Nick stood rooted to his spot, silent.

"You don't have to forgive me," she continued, her heart

battering the inside of her ribcage. "I would never expect anything like that." She paused a beat to give him a chance to tell her how awful a person she was. When nothing came, she added, "My father was very convincing and I wanted, no needed, to make him happy and gain his approval."

"Did that make you happy?" he finally asked.

"No," she said on a sharp sigh. "I've never been more miserable than when I realized I'd lost you forever and would never gain his approval. Eventually, I figured out there was always going to be a narrow path that I had to walk on to earn his love. But that took years and the damage was already done between us."

With a shirtless Nick standing close enough for her to touch him, she suddenly felt very naked underneath the bathrobe. The man was a combination of silk over steel. He was gorgeous, and caused her heart to pound wildly in her chest. Her fingertips tingled from contact with his skin. It was taking all her willpower not to close the distance between them with a small step.

Taking in a breath only served to usher in his warm, masculine scent. He was campfires and spice, all male with a powerful presence.

Before she did or said something that couldn't be taken back, she released her grip on his arm. The minute she let go, she saw the finger imprints on his muscled arm. "I'm sorry. Did that hurt?"

Nick glanced down at his arm. He shook his head. Then, he lifted his gaze to meet hers. Those beautiful eyes of his took her in when they locked onto hers. A dozen butterflies released in her stomach as awareness skittered across her exposed skin. It felt like Nick could see right through her.

"We were kids," he said in a low, gravelly tone. "It was puppy love. Nothing more."

As he turned to face her, she dropped her gaze. There was no way she could look into his eyes when she felt this vulnerable. His hand came up to cup her chin like he'd done so many times when they were younger, right before he was about to kiss her.

The lightness of his hand against her skin sent warmth spiraling through her chest, her stomach, and in between her thighs. The teenager had been a fantastic kisser. She could only imagine how much better the man had become with those thick lips—lips that parted to reveal perfectly white, perfectly straight teeth. His smile had always gotten her. The teenager could have gotten away with most anything. All he had to do was smile at her. All would be forgiven.

Of course, he'd been an amazing boyfriend. He'd been patient with her when she couldn't go out because she had to study. Even when it must have felt like she studied most of the time. He would swing by her house on his way to school just to bring her favorite coffee and steal a kiss on the front porch.

He'd spoiled her for dating anyone else with his chivalry.

Standing there, looking into Nick's eyes, Vanessa wanted to feel his lips moving against hers one more time more than anything.

"What are you thinking?" he asked in that low, gravelly voice that sent her stomach into flip-flops.

Vanessa managed a small smile. "You don't want to know."

"Try me," he said.

"Is that a dare?" she quipped, thinking she would have been better off keeping her mouth closed based on his reaction.

His pupils dilated and his smile spelled mischief. "As a matter of fact, it is. Why? Are you feeling brave?"

This was the point where she should probably say no to end this—whatever *this* was—thing going on between them. Willpower flew out the window the second he smiled at her.

"Kiss me, Nick."

10

This close, Nick needed no encouragement to dip his head down and claim those pink lips of Vanessa's. What he did need, though, was permission. Since she'd just given it, he wasted no time.

The second his mouth touched hers, a bomb detonated inside his chest. What little resolve he had left, was obliterated in the process.

Her lips parted and her tongue teased his inside her mouth. She tasted like honey and dark roast coffee, his new favorite combination.

Nick thrust his tongue deeper inside her mouth, teasing and stroking hers as his pulse raced. Their breathing quickened as her hands came up to his shoulders and then grabbed on as though needing to steady herself. He brought his up to cup her face, caressing her, positioning her mouth for better access.

He swallowed her moan of pleasure before dropping his hands to the V at the top of her robe where he hooked a finger. For a split-second, he contemplated opening her robe. It wouldn't take much. They were primed and ready to go. Nick was certain this would be the best sex of his life, which is exactly what stopped him from moving forward.

Because one question doused the burning flame...and then what?

What if they made love? What next? They would have to spend more than a few uncomfortable days together. Vanessa was in Lone Star Pass to do her job. She wasn't there for a reunion with him. Hell, she hadn't even stopped in for an apology in all these years, not that it mattered. Had he licked a few wounds over the years? Sure. Was he proud of the fact? No.

Pulling back, he rested his forehead against hers and tried to catch his breath. "This is probably a bad idea."

"The worst," she said through labored breaths. "I've missed those kisses, though."

He didn't want to let that comment go to his head. It did. Hell if he could check his ego at a time like this.

"Should we keep going?" she asked. Damn if she wasn't the definition of temptation. "We're both grown adults now. We didn't have sex when we were younger for obvious reasons. We were too young."

"You were," he pointed out. "I was a year older."

He didn't need to be able to see her lips to know she smiled at the comment. He could feel her smile.

"Technically, a year and a half," she said. "But I was stupid. You were my first kiss and you should have been my first...everything."

What was he supposed to do with that comment? His teenage self would have jumped at the chance to have sex with Vanessa. He stopped doing casual sex years ago. And that was exactly what this would be. "I keep it clear and simple, Vanessa. I don't do complicated relationships anymore."

"Shame," she said into his mouth, before she pressed her lips to his one more time in a move that caused need to well up like a tsunami.

He was going to regret turning her away. But he had to for his own sanity's sake. Losing her twice would destroy him if he let her in again.

Before things could go any further or spiral past the point of no return—they'd been too close for comfort—he took a step back.

"Coffee," he mumbled before turning away from her before he changed his mind and went for it.

Vanessa stood there like she needed a minute. It was his ego that enjoyed the fact she'd been as affected as he had by the kiss. In fact, he was certain this had just set the bar a little too high for everyone else. From now on, he'd be settling.

Then again, he wouldn't lose his mind either. Because he could lose more than that with Vanessa and his heart was no longer an option.

Nick poured another cup of coffee for him and doctored up a cup for Vanessa.

"My clothes are dirty," she said as she took the offering. The fact she'd needed to sit down at the table gave him more satisfaction than it should have. To be fair, first loves had a way of embedding themselves into someone's soul.

"I can throw in a load of laundry if you want me to wash them," he said, joining her at the table.

"That would be nice," she said. "My suitcases are at the motel on the highway."

"You could have stayed at the ranch," he said. "There's no need to stay in the motel."

"Who was I going to ask?"

"Fair point," he said.

"No one is talking to your mother any longer," she said. "When she called and my admin put her through to me, she sounded heartbroken. Or maybe it was just broken. I asked about her family and what kind of support she was receiving." She put up a hand to stop him from speaking. "No judgment here. My family is just as messed up as yours, if not worse."

"I'm guessing she said no one had been to visit her," he said, unsure if he was ready to hear any of this.

"Your father stopped by a few times in the beginning," she said.

"How did the visits go?"

Vanessa's gaze narrowed as she studied him. "Are you sure you want to know?"

Nick's cell buzzed, surprising them both. He checked the screen. "It's my father. He's outside asking if I'll allow him to come inside."

"I'd like to speak to him face-to-face," she said as she glanced down at her robe. "But this looks bad."

"He'll get over it," Nick said. "Unless it makes you uncomfortable."

"It's not like I want to change into my dirty clothes after taking a shower," she said with a determined set to her chin. "I don't have a problem with you letting him in."

Nick answered the door.

"Sorry to bother you," his father said. "I saw the lights on and figured I'd stop by to see if you were alright."

"Come in," Nick said, stepping aside. "Vanessa Mosely is here. She has taken up mother's case."

Keifer Firebrand was tall and still considered handsome for someone his age, or so Nick had heard. "Thank you for seeing me."

"I didn't hear your truck," Nick said.

"Parked it down the way," his father said as he followed Nick into the kitchen area where Vanessa sat at the table. She stood up, clamped the top of her robe shut with her left hand, and offered a handshake with her right.

His father took the offering and gave a vigorous shake, indicating his nerves were on full tilt. For months now, his father had been trying to stitch up the broken family, starting with threading a tentative bridge between him and his brother, Nick's uncle.

"Why?" Nick asked.

"Didn't want to wake you," his father said.

"Coffee?" Nick asked.

"No, thank you," his father said. "I already can't sleep."

"Why did you stop by?" Nick asked.

"Mind if I sit?"

Nick gestured to his father to go ahead. Then, he joined Vanessa and his father at the table.

"She had it rough growing up," his father began. He twisted his hands together. "It wasn't something she ever wanted you kids to know about her, but..."

His father flashed eyes at him.

"I knew something wasn't right for a long time but wanted to believe it was just my imagination," his father continued.

"How so?" Vanessa asked, leaning in with a look of compassion that was too genuine to be for show. Then again, she was a litigator doing her job.

"The drinking," he said. "I should have stopped it a long time ago."

"Why didn't you?" Vanessa continued, her voice a steady calm.

"Because I didn't know what to say," he continued. "She'd been through so much and I thought it wouldn't hurt for her to have a glass of champagne here and there. Then, she started having a glass every night, which turned into several." He issued a sharp sigh. "Rather than confront her, I turned a blind eye."

"Tell me about her background," Vanessa said, steering the conversation back on track. "What was her family life like?"

His father shook his head. "It was bad. Her therapist said she was like a flower that grew through concrete."

"My mother was in therapy?" Nick asked, unable to believe it.

"Early on in our marriage," his father explained. "Then, she stopped when we got busy having kids." His gaze locked onto Nick, which sent a cold chill racing down his back. "All of you belong to us, but we used a surrogate when your mother almost died."

"What? How? When?" This was all news to Nick.

"It was easier to hide this kind of thing thirty-plus years ago," his father said. "Plus, we lived on a ranch and could control who came and went."

"Are you going to tell me that she's not our mother next?" Nick asked.

"No, son," his father reassured. "Nothing like that. We just needed help for many of you to be born."

Nick suppressed the question he really wanted to ask, like why they even had children in the first place. He decided not to ask who was affected by this news. "Did you ever think of telling anyone about this?"

"No," his father admitted with a look of shame. "In those times, no one talked about their private business."

The Firebrands had always been a private family. But still.

∼

Vanessa didn't want to lose momentum on learning about her client, and a possible defense. "Tell me more about your wife's background. Please."

Mr. Firebrand issued a heavy sigh. "One of her uncles took advantage of her from the age of five."

Vanessa gasped. She couldn't help herself. She found herself reaching across the table to cover Mr. Firebrand's nervous hands. "That's not just criminal, it's immoral."

Mr. Firebrand nodded. Nick was silent.

"It messed with her mind," the older Firebrand said. "Especially when she confessed to her father what was happening and he told her that she must be mistaken." He shook his head. "It took her four years to pluck up the courage to speak, and she was dismissed almost immediately because her uncle was a youth minister. Her father couldn't believe his younger brother, who was so good, could do something so horrific. He decided his daughter was imagining the assaults. Blamed it on the kind of TV shows she was being allowed to watch. He was a strict, religious man. He couldn't fathom his brother hurting a child."

"Did he do anything to protect her?" Vanessa asked, now sick to her stomach. Being a defense attorney meant compartmentalizing her emotions, which was impossible in this case. She knew the victims and the affected.

Mr. Firebrand shook his head. "Your mother always had physical beauty, but it cost her sense of self-worth. She began to view herself as an object because that was the way she was treated." He hung his head. "I have to admit, I was attracted to her from the minute I set eyes on her. She was beautiful. Still is. Even after all these years."

"Your wife is a beautiful lady," Vanessa confirmed.

Finding common ground in an interview was key. In this case, she didn't have to search far. Jackie Firebrand was beautiful.

"The abuse continued for years," he said. "After being told it was a figment of her imagination, she started to think she was the one going crazy. The uncle said things to make her believe God wanted him to punish her. He also convinced her that her memory was playing tricks on her. It was a twisted scenario."

"People who abuse their position of power to damage children should never see the light of day again," Vanessa said, barely able to keep her anger at bay. She'd seen these kinds of situations more times than she cared to count. People always wonder why the victim didn't speak up or keep speaking up until someone listened. There was a simple answer. A baby elephant that is whipped in order to teach a behavior rarely ever challenges its master, not even when it was full-grown and could literally step on a human. It was conditioned not to challenge at an impressionable time. The animal never knew anything different.

Nick shook his head. "Why didn't you tell us any of this?"

"Your mother never wanted to talk about it," his father said. "She was ashamed despite knowing, on some level, it wasn't her fault."

"It would have explained a lot of her behaviors," Nick said. "Allowed us to have compassion instead of resentment."

"She was too proud." His father bowed his head. "If I could go back and do things different, there's a whole lot that I would change. The best I can do now is try to be better in the future."

"Does that include cutting your wife off financially?" Nick said, seething.

Mr. Firebrand's face twisted in confusion "What?"

"Your wife said that you cut her off," Vanessa repeated.

"Why would I do that?"

"You tell me," Nick said.

"Hold on a minute," Vanessa said. "Does that mean you didn't?"

"For better or worse," Mr. Firebrand said. "In sickness and in health. Those were the vows I made."

"The visitor's log doesn't reveal any visits from you," Vanessa pointed out.

"My wife refused to speak to me," he said. "I thought that if I gave her time, she would come to her senses. She asked for a divorce, but I knew she didn't mean it. She was trying to push me away, distance herself to keep me out of it."

The way Nick sat there, clenching his fists, it looked like he was about to explode out of his chair.

11

If only. Those two words in the context of this conversation would haunt Nick every day if he lived to be a hundred.

Nick despised secrets. Were his parents justified in keeping this from the family? Maybe. Did that change the fact he wished he'd known? One hundred percent yes. The strangest part about this whole scenario was how little he knew about his mother's life before the ranch. Then again, he didn't know a whole lot about his mother. Period.

"This explains why we never knew our grandparents on mother's side of the family," Nick managed to get out through clenched teeth. Every muscle in his body tensed at this news. He needed to exercise to work off some of the tension cording his muscles. The kiss between him and Vanessa wasn't helping matters either.

In fact, all this tension had him wanting to burn off the extra energy somehow. An intense workout. Sex. Hell, he didn't care as long as the end result was the same. He also wondered what else his parents had decided to keep from the family.

"Once again, explaining would have put your mother in the position of having to talk about the past," his father said. "It seemed easier to walk away and never look back."

"Is she really from Fort Worth?" he asked.

His father shook his head. "Corpus Christi."

"Why lie?" Nick asked.

"In case anyone ever tried to do a little digging around," his father explained. "It would make it harder to find out who she really was and where she was from."

"Were charges ever filed?" Nick asked, figuring he already knew the answer. It never hurt to ask.

"No," he confirmed. "I'm guilty too."

Nick cocked an eyebrow.

"We all play a part," he continued. "I let her sweep it all under the rug, thinking that it was ancient history. I thought if we avoided the subject altogether, it would all magically disappear and she'd be fine."

"This family has always been good at that," Nick stated, but his anger was subsiding.

"In this case, it wasn't my story to tell," his father said.

At the end of the day, his father did the right thing by respecting his mother's wishes. Nick could understand a victim needing to keep control of this much, when so much of her control had been ripped away before. "Understandable."

"We're trying to get better now if it's not too late," his father said.

The damage had been done. Could it be repaired?

"I don't know how to help my wife," he said to Vanessa when Nick didn't respond.

"The information you've volunteered today will be a huge help," Vanessa said. "It'll give us something to work with to maybe gain sympathy from a jury."

Nick's father shook his head.

"Under no circumstances are you tell anyone else what I've just told you," he said.

"I have to," Vanessa argued. "Otherwise, I have nothing to work with and your wife will end up behind bars for quite possibly the rest of her life. If I can't find a way to get twelve people to sympathize with her situation and understand why she might snap, they'll throw her in jail for the rest of her life." Her gaze bounced from Nick to his father. "You'll cripple her defense."

"She'll never speak to me again if she knows I'm the one..."

"Right now, she's in a hospital bed, bruised and beaten," Vanessa said. The words caused Nick's father to flinch. "And I have no idea what condition she'll end up in next time when she goes to a prison for hardened criminals." She blinked in disbelief. "You do understand what that means, don't you? She might never walk out of there alive. Or never walk again. Her ribs have been bruised." Vanessa reached for her cell phone and then tapped on the screen. She pulled up what looked like the doctor's report.

"Can I speak to her?" he asked.

"She's not technically allowed visitors right now," Vanessa said. "I could most definitely arrange a phone call."

"The problem is that she can't exactly speak right now," Nick interjected. His father flinched again. The man looked like he was taking blows.

While his father was there, Nick figured he should ask about the shooter.

"Any idea who might try to shoot me?" he asked.

"I heard about that," his father said before raking his fingers through thinning hair. His face dark and wrinkled from too much time in the sun. He shrugged. "If I had any information, I'd track the bastard down myself."

"The last thing I need is another Firebrand locked up in county," Vanessa warned.

His father's lips compressed into a thin line that Nick recognized as intense anger. The two of them might not have been close in the past, possibly never will be in the future. However, Nick appreciated that his father had his back. It was good to know he could be counted on when the cards were down. He'd snapped to judgment about the man not being there for his wife, Nick's mother.

"I understand," his father said, putting a hand up to calm Vanessa. "Mark my words, if anyone comes at this family, I'll take them down with my bare hands if that's all I have to work with."

"I don't need to hear you say this," Vanessa said. "And neither does Nick."

"You'd have to put him on the stand," his father deduced.

"That's right," she said. "Let's all agree to let the law do their job." She shot a look that made certain they understood and wouldn't argue. Vanessa had always been strong, and stubborn.

"You have my word," his father said with conviction.

"I'm serious," she said. "My hands are full defending Mrs. Firebrand."

"Understood." His father gave a slight nod. The way he clamped his mouth shut told Nick that his father would do what needed to be done.

"Besides, the shooter was going for me," Vanessa said.

"You don't know that," Nick countered.

"Odds are," she said. "Which is a big part of the reason I'm here right now and…" She swiped her hand down her robe as though presenting it. "Why I'm wearing this. My change of clothes is at the motel."

Nick's father studied Vanessa. Then, he shifted his gaze over to Nick, where it lingered for a few uncomfortable seconds.

"I see," he said.

Nick would put up an argument as to why this was the safest place for Vanessa right now but he'd be figured out. There would be no enthusiasm in his voice. As much as he and his father might not be close, Nick was no liar.

"Tell me more about what happened," his father said.

"There isn't much to it," Nick confirmed. "We were at the park across the street from county lockup. Morgan didn't think it was a good idea for me to drive in the state I was in after learning about Mother. So, I listened to him and headed over to the park to cool off."

"I was already there, thinking that I would give your cons time with their mother before I headed inside to speak to her," Vanessa said. "We weren't talking more than two minutes when a wild shot was fired from somewhere decently long range. Nick knocked me down to protect me, landed on top of me. The bullet nicked a nearby garbage can. Law came running out of the building. End of story."

"And they haven't caught the shooter," his father said.

"Not to my knowledge they haven't," she confirmed.

"Doesn't seem like the law is very competent," his father pointed out.

Vanessa picked up her cell and made notes in one of the apps. "Good point. How can we trust anything they say or do?"

"They've messed up the cases so far," he said. "And were unable to protect my wife while she was in their care."

"You should know that I filed a motion today to move

the trial to a bigger city," she said. "I requested Houston because I know we'll get a more sympathetic jury there."

"Would my wife be moved as well?"

"That's the idea," Vanessa said. "I'd like to get her out of here, where there's too much gossip. Folks are tried by the jury of the grapevine in these parts."

"True enough," his father concurred. "What can I do?"

"Let me set up a visit with your wife," Vanessa said. "It might be a phone call."

"Which would be better than nothing," he was quick to say.

Nick had pegged his father all wrong. Had he snapped to judgment about other people in his life too?

∽

Vanessa was finally getting somewhere in building a defense. She had Jackie Firebrand's background to work with and law enforcement incompetence. Those two factors would be powerful in the right jurors' hands.

Again, she needed the change of venue to be approved. And soon. How long before someone else got to Jackie Firebrand?

"I need to go public and I don't know how to do that without disrespecting your wife's wishes," Vanessa said, figuring she was about to get a whole heap of pushback.

"No way," Mr. Firebrand protested. "It might send her back into a depression the likes of which she may never return from."

"We have to, Mr. Firebrand. Otherwise, she might rot in a prison for the rest of her life. That is what's on the line here."

"Do it," Nick said, interrupting the headstrong battle

that was about to break out. "Do what you need to in order to keep her safe." He turned to his father. "The medical report is bad. Read it. But it's nothing compared to witnessing it. Seeing those stitches, the swelling, the black eyes." He stopped, took a deep breath. "It'll turn your stomach."

Vanessa let those words sit heavy in the air like a rain cloud before a storm.

"Okay," Mr. Firebrand finally said. "Whatever needs to happen."

"I'll do my best to get your wife's permission before I leak anything," she said. "And if I think of a better way to handle all this in the meantime, you'll be first to know."

He stood up, shook her hand and then his son's, and then said he could show himself out.

By the time he left, light was peeking through the slats in the miniblinds.

"I need to check on a few things and I should probably throw a load of laundry in," Vanessa said. She couldn't run around in the bathrobe all day.

"What's on the agenda today?" Nick said.

"Good question," she said. "Let me think about the next steps." She tapped her index finger on the dinner table. "Why can't I think straight?"

"Not enough coffee?"

"Come to think of it, I didn't finish my first cup," she said, pushing up to standing as he turned toward the machine. "I got it."

"Where are your clothes?" he asked. "I can toss them in the washer."

There was something incredibly attractive about a man who knew how to take care of himself and everyone else.

"I left them in the bathroom," she said. "And thank you."

"No problem," came before he disappeared out of the room.

The washer kicked on a few minutes later, the sound echoed from down the hall. After pouring a cup of coffee, she returned to her seat. The image of a shirtless Nick throwing in a load of laundry was sexier than it probably should be. The kiss they'd shared held so much promise. Sex with Nick, no doubt, would be the best in her life. He had a quality that made her relax enough to be herself around him. To be truly free. Finding that kind of love before her sixteenth birthday had scared the hell out of her.

Was that the real reason she'd listened to her father? She'd seen her entire law school future go up in smoke, because it would be so easy to live on the ranch with Nick Firebrand? Even now, she felt more at home here than in her own place in Houston.

Would she have thrown away her future to be with Nick? The threat had been enough to scare her into walking away and never looking back. Until now, a little voice in the back of her mind pointed out.

The annoying voice was right. She'd taken on the case, in part, because she was curious about what happened with Nick. Was he married? Did he have kids?

Not that it mattered because, despite the heat in the kiss, Nick would never take her back. Did she even want him to?

12

Dressed and ready for whatever the day brought, Nick rejoined Vanessa in the kitchen. She looked a little too right sitting there in his home. The image of her looking like she belonged here stamped his thoughts. Shoving the unproductive thought aside, he refreshed his cup of coffee.

Vanessa's gaze was intent on the screen.

"Did you decide what you want to tackle first today?" he asked.

"No," she said, "but I do have an update on your mother. The news is good. She's breathing on her own, requesting water, and the doctor is feeling good about her making a full recovery. The doctor warned it would take time, though."

"That is good news," he said. Finally, there was something to be happy about. "Is she able to talk?"

"Not much and the doctor wants her to rest," Vanessa said. "The nurse did say your mother perked up after our visit yesterday."

Vanessa glanced up as he smiled. When she smiled back, his heart danced.

It was also confused. The kiss, the passion, none of it meant anything beyond the moment. Were they still attracted to each other? The answer was clear. Yes. But that didn't mean they should act on it. The kiss had been a mistake. Well, hell, he couldn't call it that when it had felt like the most right thing he'd done in ages.

Still, nothing could come of it.

"I'm glad our visit helped," he said, redirecting his thoughts back to his mother. It gave him a whole lot of satisfaction to know he'd made a difference. Should it, though? What kind of fate would she be waking up to? His mother was going to get better so she could likely live out the rest of her life in prison. Damn. When he thought about it in those terms, it gutted him.

Hearing about her background explained a whole lot about why she drank like she did and closed herself off. She'd never once been physically abusive to Nick or any of his brothers as far as he knew. And he would have known. Someone would have mentioned it by now. Speaking of which, the others deserved to know about their mother and her background. As much as he wanted and needed to protect her privacy and right to be in charge of her own story, the others should know what was going on before the public.

Could he call a family meeting, minus Rowan? Nick couldn't blame his brother for ditching the family. Would Rowan have made the same choice if he knew about their mother?

"What are you thinking?" Vanessa asked, interrupting his train of thought.

He looked over at her only to realize she'd been studying him. "That my mother is facing a whole heap of trouble and that she also deserves to be warned before her story is out there."

She nodded.

"I knew it before," he said. "Don't get me wrong. But now? Seeing her? I realized that maybe I've been avoiding visiting her because it was going to be too hard for me to see her in jail." He put his hand up to stop her from consoling him. "That's on me."

"You're human, Nick. When are you going to realize that?"

He issued a sharp sigh. "I'm a jerk. In the worst way. I've been sitting back judging my mother for her actions, instead of trying to understand how the hell she got there in the first place."

"When the truth is being kept from you to protect you, it's not your fault that you didn't know," Vanessa argued. It was tempting to believe her, to let himself off the hook.

"I appreciate what you're saying, Vanessa. But—"

"Don't do that to yourself, Nick. You're one of the best human beings I've ever met. Believe me, in my line of work, I've been around and seen more than you can imagine. I won't let you beat yourself up. I was around back then in high school. Remember?"

He nodded. He was listening. Not that he was sold yet.

"It wasn't your job to figure out your parents or understand their demons," she said. "On the outside, your mother was cold and only cared about money. I saw it too. Everyone did. It's the reason defending her is going to be a challenge. The trial could go on because of it. Your mother has a complicated past. Your father used to be a jerk. There was no reason in the world to believe they loved you. Your dad was always too busy competing with your uncle and your grandfather was the worst of it. By leaving you and your brothers alone, your parents actually gave you a chance to decide who you wanted to be without their influence. I think that's a very good thing."

Vanessa was clearly a good lawyer. He couldn't deny the fact she made sense.

"Look at you and your brothers," she continued without missing a beat. "I can't think of better people. You all turned out to be good men. You're all honest, decent, caring individuals."

"The jury is still out on Kellan," he joked, needing to lighten some of the tension.

Vanessa cracked a smile. "Okay, definitely not Kellan. He's overbearing and bossy."

"He got a divorce," he said.

"Oh, I'm sorry," she quickly said. "I didn't know. That was awful of me to say."

"Now, he's frustrated, overbearing, and bossy," Nick teased.

They both laughed. It felt good to laugh.

"When did life get so complicated?" he asked as he leaned against the bullnose edge of the granite countertop.

"Wasn't it always?" she asked on a sigh. "It was for me, at least. I had to finish high school fast so I could get into the right college, which would lead to the right law school. I can't say that I had much of a childhood. I definitely didn't have a typical high school experience. I never even went to prom."

"No, genius," he teased. "You graduated a full year early and I couldn't ask you to my senior prom because you didn't live here any longer or talk to me once you left."

It was almost like the fun was suddenly sucked out of the room. He hadn't meant for that to happen.

"Hey, don't...I didn't mean for that to come out the way it sounded," he said to her.

She clamped her mouth closed.

"You're right though," she finally said. "I had my reasons."

"You don't have to explain yourself," he said. "We were just kids. I need to let go of all that and give you a break." He meant it. She didn't need to be reminded of what they'd shared and lost.

Vanessa studied the rim of her coffee cup before lifting it to take a sip. She set it down gently. "Walking away from you was the hardest thing I'd ever done in my life. Talking to you would have made it so much worse. You keep talking about being a bad person. How's that for selfish? I didn't return your calls because I was afraid that I'd call my mother to pick me up and come running back. Because the sound of your voice was enough to make me want to forget law school and stay right here in Lone Star Pass for the rest of my life."

"Would that have been so bad?"

"Not if it worked out," she said. "I looked at my parents' track record and wondered if that meant I was cut from the same cloth. As an adult, I see all the holes in that theory, believe me. But back then, I was convinced marriages always ended. I talked myself out of finding out what we had because we were too young for such a big love." She paused a few beats. "Did you ever think the same?"

"Yes," he admitted. "It was scary to me too. The difference being that I wasn't going to be giving anything up to be with you. And, to be honest, I never would have allowed you to give up law school if that's what you truly wanted. I was proud as hell that you graduated high school early, even if it meant I had no prom date. But those were the ideas of a kid.

No one knows if we would have worked out or even been good for each other."

"People change, right?" she asked but the question was rhetorical.

"Couples grow apart when they meet in their twenties," he agreed, despite having a feeling deep in the pit of his stomach that the two of them would have gone the distance. She was right, though. There was no way to find out without actually trying it.

"You were scared of what we had too?" she asked, looking genuinely surprised at the admission.

"I'd be a fool not to be," he confided. "You were right when you said it was a big love for such young people."

"The wild part is that if anyone could have made it work, I would have bet on us," she said. "That thought and a dime is worth about ten cents at this point."

He couldn't help but chuckle. "I won't argue there."

Not knowing if they could have gone the distance was a whole lot worse than giving it a shot and missing, in his book. Plus, who knows? They might have actually gone the distance.

～

Vanessa had a lot of regrets in her life, none bigger than walking out of Nick's life. Who knew what her life might be like if she'd turned around and come back to Lone Star Pass like he'd asked her to in his voicemails?

Being on the outs with her mother didn't help. Looking back, it was such a confusing time. If Nick came into her life now, she would know what to do with the feelings she used to have for him. Still had?

It would be impossible to have those same innocent feelings for him that she did all those years ago. The kind where her heart had known no hurt. She hadn't been jaded by experience. Their relationship had the kind of pure, innocence reserved for young loves and first loves. Her relationship with Nick fit both categories.

Since overthinking this would do absolutely no good, she switched subjects to focus on the case again. Mental breaks were normally productive. Answers to some of the most complicated questions came when she wasn't thinking about a case but focusing on something completely different.

Being here with Nick at his home, it was easy to distract herself. But probably not productive to rehash a past that was dead and buried a long time ago.

"When do you think we can pull the family together again?" she asked Nick, who'd re-entered the room after the washer buzzed, indicating the load was ready to be put in the dryer.

"I'll put a message in the group chat right now." He fished his cell out of his front jean's pocket, and then sent the text.

Was it wrong she wished he still had his shirt off?

A little voice in the back of her head reminded her of how good his skin felt underneath her fingertips.

"Thank you," she said, clearing her throat. She took a sip of coffee that had grown cold. It didn't matter. She could drink it anyway. Throw a couple of ice cubes inside and coffee houses could get away with charging at least five dollars for this.

"Done," he said with a self-satisfied smile.

"Once my clothes are dry, we should head back to the courthouse," she said. "It'll be helpful if I'm there to pressure the motions to go through."

"The judge isn't back until this afternoon," he reminded.

"How can a justice system work when the only judge is out of town?" she asked, furious. But then, *here lies a patient woman,* would never be etched into her tombstone.

"Things move at a slower pace there than in big cities like Houston," he pointed out, not that he needed to.

"Of course," she said, impatience edging her tone. "It's part of the charm of country life, but it's also incredibly frustrating when trying to get something done."

He laughed. "Ranchers start the day slow but the work is hard. I guess the rest of the community follows suit at a slower pace that never picks up like ours. Plus, another reason to move to a community like Lone Star Pass is the relative safety. Although, recent times prove otherwise."

"I read about the crime," she said. "I used to love it here. Now, I can't imagine starting my day without my latte from the corner cafe."

"You don't like my coffee?" he asked.

"No, yours is great," she said. "But I'm a latte girl, through and through."

"Sounds hard core," he said. "I'm lucky to have a regular coffee before I get started on my workday. Out there..." He motioned toward the expansive property. "I rarely have five minutes to make a cup out on the range, but when I do, campfire coffee is the best."

"I'll take indoor anytime," she quipped.

"You haven't lived until you've tasted mine over a fire."

She cleared her throat when the image of the two of them out camping like some REI commercial stamped her thoughts. "How long before those clothes dry?"

"It'll be a while, I'm afraid," he said. "How about breakfast while we wait."

"Sounds like a plan," she said. "This time, I want to help."

"You have no idea what you just signed up for, do you?" he asked.

"I'll take my chances," she said, standing up. "Plus, I actually know how to cook."

"I'm impressed," he said. "Because you used to burn popcorn."

She laughed at that, mostly because it was true.

"People change," she said by way of explanation. "And I needed to learn to cook as I've been living on my own since college."

"Cooking is a good life skill," he said. "Everyone should know how to whip up a few things in the kitchen."

"I couldn't agree more," she said. Vanessa couldn't imagine not being able to feed herself without tapping a phone app or ordering pickup. Sure, there were enough delivery services and restaurants in Houston to keep her fed, but that wasn't the point. There had always been something gratifying about knowing her way around the kitchen. Being able to satisfy a basic need to feed herself gave her a sense of pride.

Other people could do what they wanted, but she liked to cook. It relaxed her too. Mostly. There were recipes that were probably more than she should bite off literally and figuratively, and she struggled to balance all the chopping and stirring while it felt like she was standing on one foot with her eyes closed. But even those hard recipes gave her a sense of satisfaction when she conquered them.

Maybe the difference was that she wanted to do it rather than it be considered her responsibility. Everyone had a duty to feed themselves. That was as far as her belief went.

Of course, she didn't care one way or the other if

someone else made a different choice. There was a reason the popular phone app was raking in the money with delivery fees. She wasn't above using the app herself from time to time.

The pace in Lone Star Pass was different, slower than she remembered. Or maybe it was her who'd been in a rush all those years ago. Houston was supposed to be the end-all, be-all place. Then, Austin for law school but her busy life just continued at break-neck speed there. Why did the thought of sticking around after the case was over suddenly hold appeal? Stopping to smell the roses had never been so appealing. It was Nick. He made her second-guess her choices. He made her think about what was missing in her life. He made her want to stay.

13

Nick grabbed the clothes from the dryer and then supplied them to Vanessa. He waited in the kitchen for her to finish dressing. While her garments had been drying, she'd whipped up a nice breakfast of scrambled eggs and avocado toast.

"Thanks for cleaning these," she said.

"We should pick up your suitcases and get you checked out of the motel on the way to the courthouse," he said. "I'll have your vehicle towed to the ranch since it's still parked at the county jail.."

"Good idea," she agreed before polishing off the last of the coffee she'd been nursing most of the morning.

The news that his mother was doing better was a welcome relief. Nick knew better than to let himself be too optimistic. The day was still young and bad news seemed to be around most corners.

"Any word on the shooter from yesterday?" he asked Vanessa, speaking of bad news as he fired off a text to make arrangements for her vehicle.

She frowned. "They haven't caught him. The bullet

casing is consistent with a Browning X-Bolt Pro Long Range McMillan."

"A hunting rifle," he said.

"That's what the sergeant said."

"Those are pretty damn accurate from more than a mile out," he said.

"I googled it, which said the same thing. You know me and guns. I've never been good with them or cared."

He smiled at the memory of trying to take her out to shoot cans for target practice. It took three months to find a hole in her schedule big enough to take an afternoon off and hours to get her to hit anywhere near the target, even at close range. "You always had your nose in a book."

"That's true," she said, glancing over at her purse. "I'm afraid I still carry a book with me at all times. Now, though, I read for pleasure."

"When do you have time with your workload?" he asked.

"I squeeze it in when I'm at a doctor's appointment in the waiting room or taking a break while in court," she said. "Reading calms me down, especially when I'm engrossed in a good book. I'm on screens all day, so it's nice to hold a book in my hands at the end of a long day."

"Now that sounds like you," he said, his smile broadening. It was good to know some things hadn't changed.

"It's a nice distraction when I'm stuck on a case and can't seem to find a breakthrough," she said. "The solution never comes when I'm overthinking. But take my mind off the problem, and voila. My brain decides to give me what I need and then some."

"You going down a rabbit hole on a topic was never a good idea," he said, thinking back to all the times she'd end up pacing in the kitchen trying to force an answer to a case the night before one of her mock trials. "But all your dedication and focus have made you an excellent litigator."

"How do you know?" she asked.

"I've seen you in action, Vanessa. First, at the hospital. Then, with me. Next, with my father." He caught her gaze so she would know how serious he was when he said this next bit. "All that work paid off and I'm proud of you. You did it. You went after your dream and here you are."

Vanessa's smile didn't reach her eyes. "I appreciate everything you just said. It means more than you could ever know." She issued a pause. "But, I'm beginning to wonder if becoming a lawyer was ever my dream, or something I borrowed from my father's wishes for me."

"You don't love your job?" he asked.

"There are parts of it," she said. "Like when I know I made a difference in someone's life." Her smile widened. "There was a little girl who was sick but the doctors couldn't explain what was going on. Her mother seemed like a nice person. She volunteered at her daughter's school. The father was a noted radiologist in Houston. The parents were going through an ugly divorce and this eight-year-old kept getting sicker and sicker. I interviewed everyone and kept coming up empty. But then I noticed a pattern. She always continued to get worse on the weekends her father couldn't take her. She would improve a little bit when he could. Everyone chalked her sickness up to the stress of the divorce but I could sense something was going on. The little girl had no answers. She said her parents were always nice to her."

"Becoming physically sick from the stress of a family breaking up seems reasonable," he said.

"That's what everyone believed," she said. "I was starting to think that I was seeing something that wasn't there, until I found out this woman's father had died ten years earlier with similar mysterious symptoms leading up to his death. She inherited his home and a chunk of money."

Nick cocked an eyebrow. He'd read about a parent who made their child sick for the sympathy. "Munchausen Syndrome?"

"In this case, greed with her father and then revenge with her ex," she confirmed. "Turns out the mother was determined not to share the child as a way to punish her husband for leaving her. She wanted to take away the only thing he cared about, his daughter."

"That's twisted, to be able to do something like that to your own child," Nick said.

"After the discovery, we were able to find proof and get the little girl to her father, where she lives to this day," she said with warmth in her smile. "As for the woman, she will live out the rest of her life in a women's prison."

Nick couldn't imagine a mother doing that to her own child no matter what the circumstances were. It made his mother come off like a saint. "Sounds like she got exactly what she deserved."

"I think so," she said. "The important thing is that she can't hurt anyone else and the daughter is thriving with her dad." There was a melancholy tinge to her voice.

"How did you get involved in the case?" he asked. "You're not a divorce lawyer."

"No, but one of my friends is," she clarified. "He couldn't figure out what was wrong and we thought the little girl might open up to me if I was hired as a consultant on the custody case."

The twinge of jealousy he felt had no business in this conversation or anywhere else. He had a past. She had a past. Not to mention neither was tethered in any way to the other. So, this jealousy bit had to go.

"Sounds like the plan worked," he said. "Maybe you should think of doing more work like that instead of..."

He stopped himself before he insulted her relationship with her father again.

"What?" she pressed. Then came, "Oh."

Nick steeled himself for whatever was coming next. They'd made inroads on their relationship that he was afraid he'd just destroyed.

"You know what," she said on an exhale that deflated her shoulders. "You're right. I would have been a lot happier in my life if I'd figured it out myself what I wanted instead of doing what was expected of me or what made my father happy." She paused a beat, shifted her gaze toward the window over the kitchen sink. "I don't regret becoming a lawyer, but I definitely would have done everything differently."

"Like?" he asked, capitalizing on the moment.

"I would have taken my time to get through school," she admitted. "What was the rush? I don't want to end up sitting on the bench for the rest of my life, like my father hoped. I would have gone to prom." She flashed her eyes at him. "With you, if you'd asked." He definitely would have. "And then, I would have probably still finished college in three years because of all the AP classes I would have taken during high school." She laughed. "Let's face it. I'm still me."

"That you are."

There weren't many others out there like her. The mold had been broken after making her.

"But I would have had a lot more fun along the way doing normal teenager things," she continued. "I mean, seriously, what was the rush? Being in a hurry to grow up sounds like the worst of bad ideas to me from this age looking back. Why not take in each phase? Slow down. Be happy about every weird, awkward, socially inept moment of high school? Granted, I had a very different idea at the time." She cut her gaze over to him. "If I could go back and change it, I would." Another pause came. "What about you?"

~

"I don't waste time on regret," Nick said, but he had to have some.

"Are you saying you did everything right?" Vanessa asked, curious about what his response would be.

"Hell, no," he said with a lot of enthusiasm. "All I said was regret is a waste of time. Doesn't mean I don't have any."

"That makes me feel better," she quipped. "But we made it through, didn't we?"

"We did," he said with a smile that pierced her heart. "Look at us. All grown up."

"You did good, Nick."

"Yeah? So did you," he said. Those words meant the world to her. Was it possible he would consider forgiving her? Could they be friends? Not having him as part of her life for all these years was the worst punishment. "Shall we head out?"

She stood up and walked over to the sink. After rinsing out her cup, she grabbed her handbag. "Ready when you are."

Within twenty minutes, they were off Firebrand property and headed toward the highway where Vanessa had checked in the other night.

A storm had threatened. Wind had kicked up. But no rain.

On the farm road leading toward the highway, a deer

was caught underneath a branch of some kind. It blocked his side of the road. It would be easy enough to go around but he couldn't leave a wounded animal out here with no defenses. He slowed the truck to a stop.

"That poor baby," Vanessa said.

"This should only take a few minutes," he said. "I'll just need to use something as leverage to lift the branch off him without getting too close."

"What do you need me to do?" Vanessa asked, hopping out of the passenger side. She loved animals, which was one in a long list of reasons he'd been surprised she left for the city, despite knowing how much she wanted to please her father.

Nick exited the driver's side but left his truck running. He rummaged around in the toolbox, searching for something long enough to use, something strong. A crowbar would be his last resort since it wasn't quite long enough.

When he couldn't find anything that suited him, he sized up the tree that had pinned a young buck. Vanessa was off wandering through the thicket, keeping a line of sight, which he appreciated.

He joined her.

"Anything good over here?" he asked, stepping in and through scrub brush that seemed intent on choking his ankles.

"What about this?" Vanessa asked, hoisting up a long but thick branch. It had to be half a foot around and six feet long.

"Looks like it'll do just fine to me," he said, moving to her side to help walk it the twenty yards or so to the stuck deer.

"This one looks young," she said as the weary young buck watched them.

"He's barely more than a baby," Nick confirmed, hating the situation. He hoped the log hadn't done any permanent damage. If so, he'd have to come up with another plan if the buck couldn't defend himself in the wild. He'd have to capture him and take him in to the vet. Or make a call and wait. That was probably the better idea. But he was getting ahead of himself.

If they were lucky, they would free this guy and he would run off.

Nick wedged the branch in between the log and the road.

"On my count," Vanessa said, taking charge.

Before they could make another move, the sound of an engine roaring filled the air. Nick bit out a curse. Someone was inside his truck. And they were barreling right toward him and Vanessa.

"Run," he said to her after grunting and throwing his body weight into the leverage. The log popped up and the deer ran after several wobbly steps. The extra seconds spent helping the animal meant Nick wouldn't be so lucky.

The truck veered toward him. The driver was a Caucasian male. The man's sneer would be imprinted into Nick's memory until he took his last breath. Which was most likely going to be in the next few seconds.

A last-minute dive threw most of Nick's body out of the way. His left ankle caught in the tree branch, and the tire ran over it. Nick could hear if not feel the bone crunch. He bit out a string of swear words. His Ruger was inside the truck. He should have thought to bring it out with him.

Was the injured deer a trap? This was the main road he used to enter and exit Firebrand property. Since the string of recent crimes, they'd beefed up security at the ranch. Had this person been watching?

"Nick," came the shout of terror from Vanessa as the truck reversed. This bastard was coming back for seconds.

Nick managed to wrangle his foot loose but it wasn't going to do him a whole lot of good. The damn thing dangled from his ankle. If he could hop to the tree line, he'd be in better shape.

The truck could go a whole lot faster than him. Just when he thought he'd end up crushed, Vanessa came running out of the trees.

"Come get me, you sonofabitch," she shouted, waving her arms wildly in the air.

"Get back behind the trees," Nick yelled but the determined set to her chin said she wasn't having it. "Please, Vanessa."

No amount of begging could stop her. Sure enough, she drew the driver to her. The tires turned, pointing in her direction now. The driver stomped on the gas pedal, causing the tires to burn rubber as they tried to gain purchase.

A hit of adrenaline coursed through his body as he dove toward his truck as it flew past. Nick landed half inside the cab, causing enough of a distraction for the driver to release the gas pedal as he fought back.

Nick wrapped his hands around the guy's neck and squeezed with everything he had as the truck hit the branches and clunked to a stop. The engine died on the old vehicle, giving Nick his second break of the day.

The driver opened the door and threw his shoulder into it. He was almost equal in size and built like a tank. His blond hair was in a buzz cut, and framed a prison-hardened face. A prison tattoo of a woman's red lips plastered one side of his neck.

"That bitch cost me my kid," Buzz Cut managed to get out after Nick was forced to loosen his grip.

"You did that all by yourself," Nick retorted, throwing punches. A few landed on Buzz Cut's jaw, but it snapped back remarkably fast. The man was like punching a tank, fist to metal, and Nick's knuckles hurt like hell.

The door swung open, sending Nick flying. Hanging onto the side of the vehicle was not in the cards after Buzz Cut's elbow slammed into Nick's hand.

The last thing Nick remembered was his head slamming against a tree trunk.

14

Michael Trainer. Vanessa now had a name to go with the anonymous threats she'd been carrying around in her handbag. How was he out of prison?

The best way to keep the convict from killing Nick was to lead him away, deeper into the woods. Vanessa had always been a fast runner. Could she outrun this man?

Taking off in the opposite direction, she bolted toward the thicket. Who knew what kind of insects and creatures might be waiting in there, but they had to be better than Michael. The man was an animal. He'd threatened to find her when he got out. But then, most of them did.

This case was particularly heartbreaking because his daughter had been placed into foster care after the mother had been arrested for possession of a controlled substance, heroin. Jennine didn't last three months once Michael was sent away. Little Jenny, who was eight years old at the time, ended up in the hospital due to a 'farming' incident while in foster care.

The fosters who'd taken her in kept half a dozen kids to work their farm. It was a double benefit. They got paid to take the kids in, who in turn did most of the farm work. Vanessa's stomach churned when she'd uncovered all this in her investigation—an investigation that bore no fruit. Vanessa filed a motion to have the family blocked from fostering. The courts sided with the foster folks.

The threatening letters stopped six months ago. Vanessa thought the person responsible had given up and moved on. Had he been biding his time?

The ironic part about Michael going ballistic over finding out about his daughter was how much he used to abuse her and her mother. The mother had stepped in to take most of the beatings.

It had been the kind of twisted situation that had felt no-win.

Vanessa heard footsteps behind her, gaining on her as she zigzagged between the trees. If Michael had a gun—he'd gone into great detail about the many ways in which he planned to hurt her—running a zigzag pattern would be her best bet to avoid taking a bullet.

This man wanted her dead. Period. A slow, agonizing death.

If he caught up to her, her life would be over. Her first thought was that she would never see Nick again.

She hoped—prayed—that he didn't have a gun on him right now. As much as he seemed superhuman right now, he was just a man. She was capable of outrunning him. The clearing ahead was unavoidable and the lack of trees would give him time to get off a shot before Vanessa could make it across to the other side.

As it was, branches slapped her face and arms. She ran straight into a massive spider web, hoping the spider didn't come with package. Her imagination ran wild about how huge a spider had to be in order to spin a web that size as she spit and shivered.

"You'll get tired eventually," Michael said through labored breaths. He looked to have spent his days in prison working out.

"How did you get out?" she shot back, heaving. At least she'd drawn him away from Nick. Her heart squeezed at the sight of him lying on the ground, body twisted after slamming into a tree trunk.

"Clerical error," he said with a haughty laugh. "Can you believe it? Just in time for me to find you and snap your neck in half."

"How *did* you find me?"

"Linda didn't mind serving all the details of what you were up to," Michael managed to say. The footsteps stopped momentarily.

Vanessa risked a glance back. Michael was bent over, holding onto a tree and grabbing his side. The guy was all muscle, which was heavy, and less cardio, which worked in her favor. The short break gave Vanessa the break she needed to put serious distance between them before being exposed in the meadow. She sprinted, pushing her legs harder.

She wasn't mad at her administrative assistant. Linda would have protected Vanessa if she'd known what was going down.

Her thoughts immediately shifted to Nick. Was he still lying on the ground, arms and legs positioned like a rag doll? Or was he conscious? Had the law been called? There were so many dead spots out on Firebrand land. Was the farm road dead too? Could he make the call if he tried?

The pickup's engine had choked. Could it be started again? Would she make it back or die here in the thicket?

Her lungs burned as she practically leapt toward the meadow. Underbrush snagged her right foot. Instead of lifting off the ground and making it into the air, she face-planted.

Vanessa scrambled to her feet again as a chilling laugh sent ice up her spine.

"You can't outrun me," Michael sneered.

Wouldn't stop her from trying. His heavy footsteps were easy to hear as she bolted across the field of grass and wildflowers. Looking back would prove too risky. He was close enough for her to hear his labored breathing, and that wasn't good.

As her lungs clawed for air, adrenaline kicked in, giving her a much-needed boost. Guilt racked her at what happened to Little Jenny, even though being left at home with Michael and his wife could have ended worse.

Little Jenny was alive, and Vanessa was working to improve the little girl's circumstances. The legal system could be slow but she'd bet her life's work on it doing good most of the time.

As far as Michael being released based on a clerical error, Vanessa had heard of this happening before. Humans make mistakes. It happened. Thankfully, it was rare.

This time, it had unleashed a monster who'd set his sights on Vanessa. When he'd shot at her, had he intended to kill Nick? Hit her in the leg so he could fetch her and torture her?

The thought of what the man would do to her if he caught her sent more of those icy chills up her spine.

The man was far off base in coming for her. He would end up right back in jail. Then again, he'd most likely posed

NICK: Firebrand Cowboys

as another prisoner to get out. There would be a fugitive hunt, which made it even more surprising he'd tried to shoot her outside of county lockup.

Then again, some of the most successful criminals stayed right underneath law enforcement's noses. They stuck around the most obvious place when law enforcement believed they would cross state lines. Cops in other cities spent more time looking for them than their hometown police.

In her line of work, she'd seen just about everything.

Vanessa made it to the other side of the meadow without being snatched by a meaty hand, which surprised her. The heavy breath from behind her stopped too. Half afraid to glance back for what she would see, she risked a look. Realizing she had no idea how to get back, she tore off a small strip of her shirt and then dropped it on the ground.

Halfway across the meadow, Michael was bent over again. There was no circumstance under which Vanessa believed she could truly outrun or outlast him out here, unless Nick had injured the fugitive when they'd fought.

This wasn't the time to rest. She turned and ran, trying to put as much distance between them as possible.

Vanessa bit back a curse. Her purse was back at the truck. Her cell was inside her handbag. A whole lot of good that did her out here. She was lost in the thicket with only a vague idea of how to get back. Keep pressing, though, and kiss that goodbye. Nice people called her directionally challenged.

At this point, it was safe to assume Michael didn't have a gun on him. There was no doubt in her mind that he would have gotten off a shot by now. He could have had an open shot back there in the meadow.

The trees were getting thicker and thicker as she kept

running. There was no sign of running water anywhere, a trick she'd learned watching TV. It recommended finding a water source if someone was lost and following it down because it almost always led to a town.

The only positive at this point was the fact she'd drawn Michael away from Nick. Her heart ached at not knowing if he was alright. The thought of him lying there, motionless, ripped her insides out and crushed her spirit. She'd only just found him again. The thought of losing him was enough to buckle her knees.

Moving farther into the trees, Vanessa realized she could be running in circles for all she knew. She believed she was running in a straight line but there was no way to tell for certain. In the thicket, everything looked the same.

The sound of footsteps or heavy breathing coming from behind stopped. Vanessa paused to listen more carefully.

Nothing. What was she supposed to do now? Double back?

The only thing scarier than having Michael on her heels was not knowing where he was at all. The sounds of twigs crunching to her right sent her pulse racing.

∼

NICK'S HEAD felt like it was going to explode. The ringing noise in his ears was so loud, it was all he could hear. He blinked open blurry eyes, trying to get his bearings. What the hell happened?

As his eyes focused, the first thing he saw was his abandoned truck. The front tires were perched on top of a tree trunk…the scene caused total recall to come crashing down on him.

Where was she? Where was Vanessa?

With intense effort, he managed to push up to a sitting position. Leaning his back against the tree trunk, he checked both of his hands. They worked. He felt around on his head, found a serious knot on his forehead at his hairline. That was going to leave a mark.

Trying to move his legs hurt. But nothing compared to the pain in his foot.

Panic seized him when he didn't see or hear any sign of Vanessa. His foot be damned, he was going to stand. Where was his cell phone? Could he get to it and call for help?

Most of the farm road was dead cell space. It was unlikely, though possible, he might grab a bar. All he needed was one.

His cell was inside the truck. He remembered that much. There was a Ruger inside there too. He used it for shooting coyotes. It was the quickest route to get rid of a nuisance. Wild hogs were another problem on the land. He would shoot them on sight before they caused damage or attacked the herd. But now, he needed it for self-defense.

Mind wandering, he refocused on attempting to stand up. The pain was almost unbearable. No matter how severe it became, he would push on. Vanessa was out there somewhere with Buzz Cut. Her life might depend on him finding her.

The thought Nick might find her too late was a gut punch. He shook his head to remind himself he was still alive. With effort, he managed to stand up, depending heavily on his one good foot. Hopping toward his truck was the equivalent of a jackhammer against his skull. His heartbeat sounded loudly in his eardrums.

One thought prevailed...find Vanessa before it was too

late. He couldn't let himself go to a place where she was dead. Buzz Cut had been a tank. Nick could only hope he'd done enough damage to weaken the bastard. It was the best chance for Vanessa to get away.

The driver's side door was open to his truck. He pocketed the key fob. Once he was out there, Buzz Cut couldn't use the truck to get away. Neither could Vanessa. Damn. The last thought struck hard.

Buzz Cut must have a vehicle or some mode of transportation stored out here somewhere. The man must have set up on this road, waiting. The log. The deer. Props?

The setup had been a good one. Buzz Cut was cunning. A hunter? A trapper?

Between the shooting and now this, Nick would say so.

He located his cell phone on the floorboard. It had been knocked around but still worked. The contents of Vanessa's handbag had spilled all over the floorboard. Was there anything here that could be useful?

Nick didn't have the luxury of time, so he glanced around and decided there wasn't much here. Did she have her cell phone? It wasn't here. Could he call her?

What if she was hiding? What if Buzz Cut was closing in? Was her ringer off? Nick couldn't recall. The pulsing headache wasn't helping clear his mind. Calling was risky.

Checking his screen, he muttered a few choice words. No bars.

Debating whether or not to call her was useless at this point since he didn't have cell service. It didn't mean he wouldn't, though, so he sent a text to the group just in case before pocketing his phone. The branch he'd used as leverage would make a good crutch. First, he grabbed his Ruger and ammunition box. If Buzz Cut had stuck around, he would have found this. All signs were that he ran off to chase Vanessa.

Nick white-knuckled the butt of his gun. He shoved the box of ammo in his other pocket and then hopped over to the makeshift crutch. He didn't have the luxury of time to deal with his ankle.

The tree branch would help get him by. It was anybody's guess which way she would have taken off. He studied the area. A mistake at this point could send him on the wrong trail for hours.

Based on where he remembered she'd been before he headbutted the tree—and lost big time—she would have gone the route that gave her the biggest head start. Which meant toward the thicket heading east.

Moving was slower than he needed it to be. The foot couldn't take much, if any, weight. His head wasn't helping because it was next to impossible to hear anything. Heavy clouds dotted the skyline but there was no rain to be found.

Of course, this would be the moment Mother Nature decided to bring on a downpour. With Nick's luck lately, that was exactly what would happen.

He made it to the thicket and kept moving. If he guessed correctly, Vanessa would keep running in the direction she'd started to keep her advantage. She was a strong runner. Was she a match for Buzz Cut?

If Buzz Cut had a vehicle stashed somewhere, he wouldn't have gone back to the farm road. Unless he wanted to finish Nick off. Unconscious on the ground, it wouldn't have taken much.

In the battle of Nick versus his own truck, he'd lost. He bit out a few more curses as he looked for any signs he was on the right track.

Calling out to her would be a mistake. That would only

let Buzz Cut know that Nick was not only alive but making his way through the thicket in the hopes of finding them. Besides, if Buzz Cut got to Vanessa first, it would only give him the advantage.

At this point, the man wouldn't want to leave any witnesses and Nick could identify the bastard in a lineup. Until Buzz Cut was safely behind bars, neither Vanessa nor Nick would be safe.

Nick took the threat very personally.

He kept pushing despite the pain, checking his phone every few minutes. After what felt like forever but was probably more like ten minutes, he saw a meadow up ahead.

Which way would Vanessa have gone? Would she have gone for it, running out in the open? Or would she have cut left or right?

It would depend on whether or not Buzz Cut had a gun and how close he was to catching her, if she'd made this far. He couldn't ignore the possibility Buzz Cut killed her and dumped the body somewhere.

The chilling thought slammed into Nick. Hope was all he had, so he decided to proceed assuming that Vanessa was alive, until proven otherwise.

And then he saw it. A small strip of her cloth on top of the scrub brush. What the hell?

The material matched the shirt Vanessa had on. Did she drop this here on purpose? A breadcrumb?

Nick checked his cell. Still, no coverage.

At least he had a clue. Vanessa had been here. Was she trying to talk to him?

With renewed hope, he looked ahead at the meadow. Buzz Cut could be anywhere. Hell, he could be hiding around the edge, waiting for Vanessa to return, thinking she would backtrack to the truck at some point. The theory supposed she'd outrun Buzz Cut. The man was thick and built. Guys like him carried a lot of weight in their chest and arms. They could bench press like a mug, but they didn't generally make good runners. She could have escaped.

Nick clung to the first sign of hope he'd had since coming to.

15

Was Vanessa moving in circles?

Every sound, every time a twig snapped, panic shot through her. As much as she wanted—needed?—to know if Nick was alive, going back to the truck seemed like the worst of bad ideas.

What if Michael circled back already? What if he gave up on finding her and decided to wait her out back on the farm road? It stood to reason that she would have to make her way back there at some point. Was he one step ahead?

Not to mention, Nick might still be there. He wouldn't leave. Not without finding her first. If she was certain of one thing, it was that Nick wouldn't abandon her out here. Which led to another problem. If, by some miracle, he was up and around, he would be searching for her.

Would he run into Michael first?

She ripped off another piece from the hem of her shirt, and then dropped it onto the ground. This might also be a bad move, but she had to do something. Plus, she was lost. If she came across a strip of her shirt, she would know she'd been there before.

NICK: Firebrand Cowboys

Adrenaline had worn off long ago, so she felt every ache and pain at this point. Constant concern over Nick had her stomach churning to the point she could vomit.

And Michael was out there somewhere. He could literally be anywhere.

Vanessa wished she had her cell phone with her. There had to be bars out here somewhere that she could find. Being able to call for help would make all the difference in the world.

A twig snapped. It was probably just another animal like it had been the last dozen times she'd stressed out. At this point, was it safer to stay put? Move to a place either higher up on a tree branch or hide underneath one of the fallen trees. The thought of bugs crawling all over her made her involuntarily shiver.

But if it had to be done.

Climbing would help from a vantage point perspective. However, if spotted, there would be nowhere to go. So, the fallen tree would offer the best protection and give her an escape route. Okay, then. She swallowed her fears best as she could and moved quietly to the nearby tree on its side. Decaying. The main problem with this plan is that someone could come up from behind. She would have no protection.

Another twig snapped. The animal was getting closer. Shouldn't it be going in the opposite direction?

Fear struck, causing her to hide. She crouched down, making herself as small as possible. A white shirt probably wasn't her best move but she'd had no idea what the day would hold. If she'd known she was going to be out here in the woods, she would have chosen colors that blended in.

Hunger was probably making her delirious. Her thoughts were bouncing all over the place. Another thought struck. What was her plan if she ended up stuck out here for the night? Given her directional challenges, it wasn't just possible but it was likely.

The twig snap wasn't far away. Could she risk a glance?

Heart thundering in her chest, she tried to hold her breath as something moved past. She didn't dare look up, not now. Instead, she stayed as small as possible, reciting a protection prayer she'd learned as a little girl.

A slow whistle sent a shockwave through her system. This had to be Michael. If Nick had managed to come to and somehow anticipate which way she'd gone, he likely wouldn't be this close.

The whistle couldn't be more than twenty feet away unless the wind carried it. How confident did the bastard have to be in order to walk through the woods whistling?

Anger roared through her. As much as she wished she could let him have a piece of her mind, silence meant the difference between staying alive and a slow, awful death. Vanessa tried not to breathe.

"Come out, come out, wherever you are," Michael's voice was filled with the kind of boastfulness and overconfidence that made her skin crawl. The sound was like icy fingers gripping her spine, spreading the chill through her body like a virus.

Vanessa tried to breathe as quietly as possibly, praying he couldn't hear the thunder of her heartbeat as strongly as she could.

The sound of underbrush being shaken sent her pulse racing. He was close. Too close? At this point, could she get away if she needed to?

This must mean bad news for Nick. Michael wouldn't have left the scene if he feared Nick would make a recovery. She wanted to scream but knew better than to make a sound. It was possible Michael could walk right past. Once he moved a safe distance into the thicket, she could double back.

A sobering thought struck. She could end up walking in circles until Michael found her or she starved to death, if an animal didn't get to her first. There were cougars and feral pigs in these parts that could shred her. But her biggest threats came from smaller creatures. Creatures like rattlers, copperheads, and diamondback snakes, just to name a few.

Even smaller than those but just as deadly were scorpions, black widows, and brown recluse spiders. The water wasn't any safer in these parts, considering alligator sightings were becoming more common. Granted, attacks were rare but she couldn't rule out the risk. She would have to stay alert.

If she got lost for days, dehydration would kill her before she starved to death. Neither of which sounded appealing.

So, basically, as much of a threat Michael was, he only scratched the surface of things that could kill her out here if she was left to her own devices for long.

Banging a stick or something he'd found into larger scrub as he walked, she was able to track his movement. He'd gone past her now but was still close enough for her to hear the banging.

And then it stopped. Could she trust it? Or was this a trick?

Vanessa risked a glance in the direction where she'd last heard the noise. Nothing stirred and she didn't see Michael. It was too soon to celebrate or relax.

On full alert, she peeked again. This time, she gave herself a chance to survey the area. There was no sign of him. Was it safe to guess that he would continue on in the same direction? Or would he double back?

Stay here and he might find her. Leave and the noise she

would inevitably make could alert him to her presence. Just because she didn't see him didn't mean he wasn't there. He'd been wearing a dark shirt and pants, and would blend into the elements to a certain degree.

Could she go? Or maybe a better question was whether or not she could afford to stay. The few strips of ripped clothes might help her find her way back to the farm road. At the very least, they could tell her if she was on the right track.

Since there was no sign of Michael, she had to take a chance. Not knowing if Nick was alive or if she could help him was eating at her.

Vanessa listened closely. All she could hear was the sound of the wind, which was picking up speed. Storm clouds rolled across the sky, hiding the sun. Without her phone, she had no idea what time it was. Her stomach growled despite its churning.

Food would probably make her sick anyway.

As far as Michael went, there was still no sign of him. Unsure when another moment like this would present itself, she bolted back where she believed she'd come from making as little noise as possible.

The increasing winds would provide some cover for the sounds she made. She could say the same about Michael. But staying put didn't guarantee her safety either. The *now or never* mentality might get her in more trouble, but at least she didn't feel like a sitting duck any longer. Not doing anything in the face of danger was the worst feeling.

At least now she was on the move. For better or worse.

∼

THE OVERWHELMING LIGHTHEADEDNESS engulfing Nick

wouldn't deter him from staying the course. Vanessa was too important. Slow or not, he would methodically make his way through this entire wooded area until he found her.

Nick knew these lands like the back of his hand and this area was expansive. A person could easily get lost here. Since Nick had never seen Buzz Cut before, he figured the bastard wasn't from around these parts, which meant he was after Vanessa. The fact that he went after her before finishing the job with Nick told him everything he needed to know about the man's intentions.

Winds kicked up, making it difficult to hear anything over the gusts. All indications said a storm was brewing, but this was Texas and weather could change on a dime.

Movement ahead caught his attention. He couldn't see clearly from this distance, and the fact that he had to shield himself by hiding behind the nearest tree trunk. Nick palmed the full-size officer-style Ruger in a .45 automatic. The lightweight aluminum was cool against his sweaty hand. He liked this .45 automatic for its light trigger pull. The reset was quick and responsive, and its accuracy got the job done quickly and efficiently without the need for a second shot. All that was required was a decent sharpshooter, which he was.

Having grown up on a ranch, he'd been taught how to handle a weapon from an early age. He'd hunted poachers and had to shoot threats to the livestock like feral hogs and coyotes who came dangerously close to the main house.

He studied the area where he'd seen movement a few seconds ago. Could have been the wind whipping something around. He reached in his pocket for the strip of cloth from Vanessa's shirt, rubbing the material in between his thumb and forefinger.

Tucking the material inside his pocket, he kept watch

ahead. Nick hoped touching the cloth would bring better luck in finding her. Was he being superstitious? Yes. He was also desperate and feeling himself get weaker by the minute.

His vision blurred as a fog settled over his brain. And then he saw a streak of red hair.

"Vanessa," he whispered, hoping he'd been loud enough for her to hear him.

Nick took a step forward. His legs gave out. He landed with a hard 'thunk.'

The headache was almost blinding as he tried—and failed—to sit up. The next thing he knew, Vanessa's singsong voice was next to his ear.

"Wake up, Nick," she said, but he was almost certain that he was imagining her.

Until a few gentle pats on his left cheek got his attention. Instinctively, he grabbed her wrists as he forced his eyes to open.

"Stay with me, please," she continued, her forehead creased with worry.

"I'm here," he said. The words came out in a whisper despite him trying to speak in a regular tone.

"Good," she said with a smile that caused his chest to squeeze. "Where does it hurt the most?"

"I'm fine," he reassured.

She shot him a look.

"Okay, I'm not doing all that hot," he said. "My head feels like a grenade exploded inside my skull and all that's left are a dozen jackhammers going full tilt. I can get past that because I've had headaches in the past, but the bones in my foot are broken and my ankle looks more like a grapefruit which I'm almost certain will be a watermelon if I keep putting weight on it."

"Have you called for help?" she asked, but a noise to

their left had her jumping to attention before he could answer.

"What is it?" he whispered, forcing himself to twist around so he could get a visual.

A few seconds of silence passed that felt like an eternity as he watched, looking for any hint of movement. Looking for Buzz Cut. With a storm brewing, there was plenty of activity.

"Nothing," she finally confirmed. "Leaves and wind."

Nick managed to lean against a tree trunk for back support. "Where is he?"

"I'm not totally sure," she said. "He was chasing after me but, thankfully, I'm a decently fast runner."

"Where did you lose him?" Nick asked, needing to assess the situation. Getting all the facts was the first step.

Her gaze widened as she shrugged. "I'm not sure how long ago it was exactly. I've been winding through the woods, trying to get back to you for at least ten minutes."

A ten-minute head start wouldn't buy them a whole lot of time considering Nick's injuries. Should he send her back alone? She could make it back to the farm road, possibly flag someone down. He could give her one of the phones. She was more mobile than him, so she could find bars and call for help.

Nick locked gazes with her because she needed to see how serious he was about what he was about to say. He opened his mouth to speak, but clamped it shut the minute she gave him 'that' look. The one that said he was about to be wasting his breath.

"I won't consider breaking up now that we've found each other again," she said, pre-empting what he was about to suggest.

Since he knew better than to argue with a lawyer, he

said, "I have two cell phones and a gun. I also have injuries that are going to slow us down considerably."

"On the positive side, you also have intimate knowledge of this area and, therefore, are quite possibly the only one who can get us out of here alive," she pointed out.

"Which way was he headed?" Nick asked.

"He was still going in the opposite direction we are now," she said. So, they had more than ten minutes.

"The truck is no good," he said, "The engine is flooded."

"What about cell service?" she asked. "There have to be spots out here where we can pick up a signal."

"It's possible," he said. "To be honest, I'm not on my cell when I'm in the woods. And I haven't been out here in ages since I started working full-time with the cattle. I guess you could say that I get enough outdoor time working the ranch. The only other place I go is fishing and that's on the other side of the property."

"What about now?" she asked.

Nick handed over her cell and then checked his screen. "I've got nothing."

"Hold on," she said, standing up and moving around. "I might have a bar."

16

Vanessa stopped at the exact spot where she caught a faint bar. She hit those magic call for help three numbers on the keypad and then brought the cell to her ear. Nothing.

Disappointed, she shook her head.

"We might get lucky on the walk back," Nick said. "Plus, I know a way around. It'll take us out of the way but hopefully make it more difficult for...who is he?"

"Michael Trainer," she supplied, helping Nick stand. "I helped put him away and ensure he lost all parental rights to his daughter. The mom ended up not being an option, his girl went into foster care and was hurt. I got anonymous letters for a while."

"I'm guessing the letters were threatening," he said.

"Yes," she said. "I would have turned them over to the judge but there was no proof he was the one actually sending them. I knew it was him. He knew that I knew. I guess he wanted me to be scared."

"Wasn't he in prison?" How did he get the letters out?" he asked.

"There are ways when someone is determined," she pointed out.

"Do you get a lot of threats in the course of your work?" he asked as they started the slow trek back. He motioned for them to go wide. She worried he wouldn't make it all the way back. As it was, he had to lean some of his weight on her.

At least they had some means of protection now. The Ruger tucked in the waistband of his jeans would stop Michael in his tracks. Plus, Nick knew the area and could get them back to the farm road. Breaking off on her own wasn't something she would consider once she found him. Getting lost wouldn't do either one of them any good. This way might be slower, but it guaranteed they would find their way.

Plus, being together helped keep her nerves a notch below panic. Being with Nick always had a way of calming her fried nerves and bringing a sense of calm over her like none she'd ever known. It had been the same all those years ago too. She'd been too young to know how rare and fleeting the feeling was, or that she would live into her early thirties without finding it again. At least, not until now.

"I get some threats," she said. "The ones I defend and win are generally very happy with me but there are cases with spouses that get ugly. Domestic disturbance is one of the most dangerous calls for police officers to go on for a reason. Tempers flare when it comes to matters of the heart."

"I can imagine," he said. "And I've heard that about domestic disturbance calls."

"There are plenty of folks out there who threaten," she continued. "Acting on it is rare. Usually folks calm down after spending a while in jail. When they are released, the last thing they want to do is be sent back."

"Except this guy," he said.

"Michael is out early due to a clerical error," she informed. "He shouldn't be on the streets at all." She shook her head as they made their way toward freedom, step by step. "He has nothing else to lose."

"The system is broken," he said. "It's a damn shame because when that happens, a child suffers at the hands of adults who are supposed to protect them."

"It's enough to anger anyone, except in this case," she said. "Michael's mistake is not pointing the finger at himself. If he was the husband and father that he was supposed to be, none of this would have happened. We wouldn't need courts to intercede, take away rights, or tear children away from their families."

"Is that part of the reason you never want to have kids?" he asked, surprising her with the change in topic.

"I guess so," she said. "I never really thought about it like that though."

"You've seen a lot," he pointed out as they inched their way, checking every few steps to make sure they weren't being followed.

"Too much, I guess," she confirmed. "Between that and my own parents' marriage, I guess I figured that I'd only destroy a child's life."

"You wouldn't," he said.

Those words were dangerous because they awakened a desire in her that she'd never felt before. Because she could see herself having a family with Nick.

"How do you know?" she asked, curiosity getting the best of her.

"I've known you for a long time," he said. "You have a

stubborn streak a mile long. You would dig your heels in and make sure you were a good parent to a child, or you wouldn't have one. It's as simple as that."

"Not having one has been the plan so far," she admitted. He was right about the stubborn bit. She could acknowledge it. When used properly, it made her determined to win a case or find a breakthrough. It was the part of her that wouldn't let her give up no matter how difficult a case seemed on the surface.

"You might change your mind someday," he said, wincing with every step. "Any kid would be lucky to be yours."

Those words spoken by him were enough to melt her heart and her resolve. She should definitely not spend too much time with Nick. Because he made her believe certain things were possible that she'd never wanted in a million years before him.

"This Michael person has nothing to lose," Nick pointed out.

"That's right," she said. "He's going back to jail no matter what and he lost his daughter, so he'll never get her back. He doesn't know where she is because we had his parental rights revoked for when he was released, which was supposed to be years down the road."

"A clerical mistake means there's most likely a manhunt going down right now," Nick said.

"If we can get him out in the open, we have a chance that law enforcement will do the rest for us," Vanessa said.

"He knows that too," Nick said. "Which is why he set up out here where there's fewer law enforcement officers. You coming here created the perfect storm for him to isolate you."

"My assistant gave him the information to find me here,"

NICK: Firebrand Cowboys

she said. "Linda had no idea what she was offering. And I'm certain he was cunning enough to smooth talk her right out of the data."

"How long has he been locked up?" he asked.

"Two years," she said. "Of a ten-year sentence."

Nick stumbled and she barely kept him on his good foot.

"Maybe we should take a break," she said.

He shook his head. "I'm fine. We can keep going."

"Are you sure?" she asked, wishing she could find bars for his phone.

"We don't have a choice," was all he said. "Besides, the faster we get to the road, the quicker we can get help. This bastard needs to be locked up again so he can't make threats or hurt anyone else."

"You won't get any argument out of me."

"Maybe you should stop, like the bitch said," Michael's voice boomed from behind them.

∼

NICK SPUN around on his good foot, winced at mind-numbing pain, and tucked Vanessa behind him. Buzz Cut, a.k.a. Michael, stood there, feet spread apart in an athletic stance with the barrel of a gun aimed at them.

He managed to lean over a step or two in order to shield them with trees that were staggered in between them and the shooter.

This wasn't good. Nick's vision was already blurring. Pain had him wanting to pass out, but he'd managed to fight the urge so far. A thump of adrenaline would come in handy about now except that he might have drained the supply.

Or maybe a steady supply was the only thing keeping him standing and this was as good as it was going to get.

"Hands where I can see 'em," Michael ordered. The bulk of his body mass was behind a tree as well. Smart guy. He'd used a hunting rifle the other morning. A couple of years in jail could make anyone rusty, but Nick wouldn't take the guy's aim for granted.

He lifted his hands in the air, palms out.

"Now send her over to me," Michael demanded.

"Afraid I can't do that," Nick stated, stalling for time. He needed to think of something to deter the man and keep him from shooting. Make no mistake about it, Michael intended to kill them both. He had no plans to allow either one of them to walk out of this thicket alive.

The crack of a bullet split the air. A splinter of wood came flying off the tree near Nick's head.

"Are you okay?" he whispered to Vanessa, turning his head slightly while keeping his gaze firmly fixed on Michael.

"Yes," she confirmed. "I'm not hit."

He breathed a sigh of relief.

"Hands up, bitch," Michael shouted to Vanessa.

"You're disturbing the wildlife," Nick said, throwing anything out there that came to mind to stall so he could think of how the hell they were going to get out of this.

He felt hands on his back and then the Ruger slipping out of his waistband. Vanessa wasn't used to guns. Aiming while adrenaline surged was a whole different ballgame anyway. If she tipped their hand without getting off a shot, they'd lose the element of surprise.

At this point, Michael didn't know they had a weapon. He'd like to keep it that way, if at all possible.

Another shot fired, a little closer this time.

He felt Vanessa tense up behind him.

"It'll be okay," he said out of the side of his mouth.

"What was that?" Michael shouted. "I didn't hear you."

"Wasn't talking to you," Nick said, doing his level best to remain calm and not let his own temper get in the way of good judgment.

And then before he could figure out anything else to say, Vanessa bolted right into thicker trees.

Michael followed her movement with the barrel of his gun, took aim, and fired.

The bullet pinged a tree in front of her. She flinched but kept moving until she disappeared.

"Follow her and I'll track you down," Nick warned. "You have me right here. She'll come back. Don't do anything stupid."

If Michael ran, there wasn't anything Nick could do about it. He wasn't strong enough to follow. Hell, he was barely making it out of the woods at a snail's pace.

But Michael didn't know that.

Nick fished out his cell phone and held it out in front of the tree. "The law is already on its way."

"Like hell it is," Michael shot back.

"Believe me, it is," Nick said. "Pretty soon, choppers are going to fill the air. Deputies, cops, and canines are going to fill these woods to track you down. You can't get away."

Michael glanced side-to-side. The words were getting to him. He was nervous.

"I have to," he said. "Once this bitch is dead, I have to rescue my Little Jenny. And Vanessa Mosely is going to tell me where my daughter is. I know she knows."

Just then, Vanessa popped out from behind a tree to their left, and got off a shot. She'd either been going to target practice or had beginner's luck because the bullet slammed into the hand holding the pistol.

Instinctively, Michael grabbed his injured hand while

the gun went flying into the scrub brush. He dove for it, exposing more of his body mass.

Vanessa took aim and shot him in the upper thigh. Nick hobbled over in time to throw himself on top of Michael. Off the bad foot, he could pin the bastard to the ground.

"Go get help," Nick instructed. "Find cell service and bring someone back."

Vanessa started off but then doubled back. She picked up the branch Nick had been using to help himself walk and slammed it into the back of Michael's head. His body went limp as he was knocked unconscious.

"I'll be right back," she promised.

Nick fell in and out of consciousness as he waited for what seemed like an eternity. By the time emergency personnel and law enforcement arrived, he was slipping away as Michael was waking up.

Good. The bastard needed to be fully awake when he was arrested.

Then, everything went black.

～

NICK WOKE up in a hospital room with Vanessa right by his side. His brothers and a few of his cousins were there, forming a circle around the bed. His father stood off to one side.

"Hey, you're awake," Vanessa said. Looking at her first thing was like a campfire on a cold night. "Surgery on your foot went well. You'll be in a boot for a while but should fully recover."

The news was good. He managed a smile as he searched the faces in the room, all but Rowan's. Smiles broke out as well as a collective sigh of relief.

"We knew you'd make it through alright, but dang, did you have to give us a scare?" Kellan asked with a smirk. "Haven't we been through enough already?"

"Just keeping everyone on their toes," Nick said, hearing the raspy quality to his own voice.

"We'll be in the hallway if you need us," Morgan said before, one by one, they filed outside after gazes bouncing from him to Vanessa.

"Everything okay?" he asked Vanessa.

"Yes," she said, her tone unreadable. "I think they just want to give you some breathing room. Your mother is doing better and my motions to have the trial relocated worked out. Looks like I'm heading back to Houston tonight."

"Do you have to go?" he asked, figuring he already knew the answer to the question. And he'd be damned if he put his heart on the line a second time for it to be stomped. "You know what? On second thought, don't answer that question. I appreciate everything you've done for me and for sticking around the hospital while I got through surgery. You can go now. You've done your part."

Vanessa stood up and took a step back almost as though he'd thrown a punch. "I drove myself here. Thanks for delivering my car to the ranch, by the way. I can leave now."

"I wasn't trying to hurt your feelings," he clarified. Of course, she would leave. She always left.

"Is that what you want?" she asked with a hurt look that almost had him back peddling. "For me to go?"

"Maybe it's best if we take a little time off of each other," he said, suddenly feeling sick to his stomach. "Feelings have been stirred up and it's probably best if we take a minute to figure out what that means." The last part was true enough, but the words came out like sandpaper on his tongue.

Her chin quivered and her gaze darted out the window.

Now, he really wanted to puke. The queasy feeling took hold and didn't let go. The fear he'd just ruined the best thing that had ever happened to him pierced his heart, making it hard to breathe. A familiar ache settled in his chest. It was the one he recognized from all those years ago when he'd lost her the first time.

"If that's what you want," she said before walking out as he tried to call her back to the room and apologize.

Had he just royally messed up?

17

"You have a package."

Vanessa glanced up to find her administrative assistant at her office door. Linda Larson waved when the two made eye contact. Vanessa had been so deeply entrenched in the file she'd been staring at on the screen that she hadn't even heard a knock.

"Come in," Vanessa said, waving her assistant in.

Linda carried in a sizable flat rectangular box. It couldn't be flowers, obviously. She set it on top of the desk. "It's not heavy." Linda made eyes. "I wonder what's inside."

"I'm guessing there's a card or something to indicate this belongs to me," Vanessa said, drawing a blank as to who might have sent it and why. She glanced at the time. "It's seven o'clock on a Saturday night. I didn't realize FedEx delivered this late on a weekend."

"This one was hand delivered," Linda supplied.

Vanessa's cell buzzed. She glanced at the screen as she sat a little straighter in her executive office chair. The text was from Nick. They hadn't spoken in days. Each was supposed to be taking time to hit the reset button before deciding their next steps, if any.

"What the...?" Vanessa asked out loud as she read the text from Nick telling her to open the box.

She set the phone down and then tugged at the big red bow on the box.

"I can't wait to see what's inside," Linda said, clasping her hands together against her chest while giving a little hop of joy. Her smile was a mile wide.

Vanessa cocked an eyebrow at her assistant. "Do you promise you had nothing to do with this?"

"Are you kidding?" Linda asked. "I'd never be able to keep this a secret."

That much was probably true. Linda was a sweetheart, but the term chatterbox came to mind. She was also an open book. There were no secrets with Linda unless they related to a client or a case. Then, she was a vault. They'd already had a talk about Linda never handing out information about Vanessa's whereabouts no matter who asked after Michael's arrest.

"Okay, I should probably stand up." Vanessa did as she repositioned the box before removing the lid. The red ribbon tumbled onto the floor. She made a move to catch it a second too late. Sparkles inside the box caught her attention. "Holy, Batman, what is this?"

She gingerly picked up the purple gown. Underneath the folded sequined evening gown was a pair of designer spiked heels. Vanessa held the beautiful evening dress up against her.

"It's a perfect fit and you're going to look gorgeous in it," Linda said, gushing.

"Thank you for the lovely compliment," Vanessa said, certain she was blushing. Compliments always made her feel self-conscious for some odd reason.

"You should definitely text him back," Linda urged.

"I plan to," Vanessa said, still taking in the stunning gown. She had no idea where she would wear the dress out to but that didn't stop her from appreciating the gesture.

She set the gown gently on top of the box and then bent down to pick up the ribbon.

"Or you could just tell me face-to-face," the familiar male voice said—a voice that rolled over her and through her, causing desire to well up.

Vanessa was dreaming. Of course, she was. This was all an elaborate fantasy that she was going to wake up and realize wasn't real any minute now. She blinked her eyes a couple of times.

Nope. She was wide awake.

From underneath the desk, she could see a shiny black dress shoe and a black sock in a boot. Her heart fluttered, skipping a few beats as she slowly stood up and Nick came into view. The tuxedo he wore made him look sexy as sin. Thick mane slicked back, the man was the definition of gorgeous. Tall, muscled, and in a tux, Vanessa's pulse raced as she took in the sight of him.

"I'll be out here if you need anything else," Linda said, a full blush to her cheeks as she stood beside Nick.

"You can go home for the night, Linda," Vanessa said. "I doubt I'll be getting any more work done."

"You're the boss," Linda said before taking a step back. She practically beamed at Vanessa while giving her a solid two-thumbs up.

If Nick turned his head in the slightest right now, Linda would most likely die from embarrassment.

"Go home," Vanessa mouthed, shaking her head.

Linda kept up her antics until she disappeared down the hallway.

"Is she finished?" Nick asked with a smirk.

"Doing what?" Vanessa asked, trying to be coy.

"I saw her reflection in the glass hanging on the wall," he said, smirk firmly in place.

"She would absolutely die if she knew you saw that," Vanessa said with a laugh. Her expression turned serious. "I wasn't expecting you tonight. How long has it been since we last spoke?"

He made a show of glancing at his watch. "Four days. Eleven hours. And thirty-six minutes."

"Did we make plans that I seem to have forgotten about?" she asked, motioning toward the box.

"Put the dress on and we'll see," he said with an irresistible twinkle in his eye. That look sparkled with adventure.

"Should I be afraid?" she teased.

"Of me?" he asked, feigning hurt. "I'm shocked." He put a hand to his chest like he was in the middle of a heart attack. "And hurt."

"I'll put on the dress if you stop acting like a cut-up," she quipped.

He regained his composure in a flash. He wiped a hand down the front of his jacket like he was getting rid of lint before he took a seat. "I'll wait."

Vanessa couldn't help but smile. She couldn't remember the last time she was genuinely surprised, in a good way. She grabbed the gift and then headed into the bathroom. Thankfully, she kept a makeup bag in there just in case she worked right up until she ran out for a dinner date. It had happened more than she cared to admit. For one, she worked all the time. And, secondly, she couldn't remember the last time she'd been so excited about a date that she'd gone home first to spend time primping.

Slipping out of her work clothes, she glanced in the mirror. A little bit of mascara and some lipstick should do the trick. She had a black sequined hair tie from the Hope Gala, a charity event that raised money benefiting orphans.

Sliding her feet into the shoes felt like a true Cinderella moment, which was a big statement considering she'd never subscribed to the whole fairy tale fantasy. And yet, there she was standing in front of a mirror with her hair pulled back off her face in an incredible gown, feeling like a princess.

When she opened the door and stepped into the room, the look on Nick's face nearly knocked her back a step. He immediately stood up, and his gaze roamed her curves.

"Wow," he said, eyes wide. "You're even more beautiful."

"You're not so bad yourself," she said, trying and failing at pulling off a casual demeanor. Seeing him standing there in her office in a tuxedo no less had her heart hammering against her ribcage. "It's good to see you, Nick."

"You too," he said.

"Now, do I get to know where you're taking me?"

"It would ruin the surprise," he said, his voice low and gravelly. Sexy.

"I thought *you* were the surprise," she countered, clearing her throat from the sudden dryness. "You did show up here unexpectedly. Bearing gifts, no less."

He closed the distance between them, and then took her hands in his. "Do you trust me?"

This close, she could smell his spicy aftershave as she breathed. The heady scent would make her agree to pretty much anything. "Yes."

"Good," he said. "We need to lock up because we're getting out of here."

Vanessa gathered her purse and closed down her system. She locked up behind them as they exited the building from the side door.

There, waiting, was a stretch limo.

What in the world was he up to?

~

NICK HAD EVERYTHING PLANNED OUT. Pulling this together on short notice had been quite a feat. He could only hope Vanessa liked it because he had a lot to make up for after the foolish move he'd made in the hospital.

Tonight, as always, she had the kind of beauty that took his breath away.

"Hold on, okay?" he said, as she turned to face him. His heart took a hit at her beauty, inside and out. True beauty showed through the eyes. There was something about the eyes being the window to a soul that rang true to him. Hers was pure and kind despite sometimes needing to put up a tough front.

"Okay," she said.

"Close your eyes," he instructed. She did.

Nick hobbled to the passenger seat of the limo. The driver, Alec, rolled down the window so Nick could retrieve the corsage. By the time he returned to Vanessa, she was peeking. Her wide smile said she was happy.

"You can open your eyes all the way now," he said on a chuckle.

Vanessa did. "What is this for?"

"Vanessa Mosely, will you go to prom with me?"

She stood there momentarily speechless, which was a surprise given her line of work and natural ability to talk at pretty much any moment. "Are you serious?"

"I'm asking you to prom," he confirmed, holding out the corsage. "What do you say?"

"Nick, I don't know what to say," she said as a tear streaked down her cheek. He reached up and thumbed it away.

"Then, say, 'Yes,'" he said.

"Yes," she confirmed, bringing her hand up to cover her mouth. He caught her by the wrist to put her corsage on. Then, he ushered her into the back of the limo. "I don't have a flower for you."

"Not necessary," he said, producing one from the small fridge in the limo where he'd been keeping the single red rose fresh.

She pinned it on his lapel with shaky hands. "Where are we going?"

He tapped the button on the intercom. "Let's roll."

Alec acknowledged the instruction before proceeding to the local high school where Nick had managed to rent out the gym for the night. A party planning group made sure there was a DJ. They decked the place out.

"This is beautiful," Vanessa remarked as they pulled up alongside the exterior gym doors that were wide open.

"Enchanted evening is the theme, according to the party people I hired," he informed, his chest puffed out with pride that she was in awe. He exited the limo first, and then held out a hand to help her.

Vanessa stepped out, and then stood there like she was taking it all in.

Lights were strung and the place resembled a wonderland. The smile on her face was all he needed. She deserved to be happy. Someone should strive to bring out that smile every day.

She took his arm, and they walked inside.

"This has to be the best prom in the history of proms," she said.

He laughed. "I sure hope so."

A few tables were sprinkled around the room. A long table sat to one side, filled with punch that was spiked. What could he say? He wanted her to have the full experience.

Two of his brothers and four of his cousins filed in a moment later, all in formal wear.

Vanessa turned around and clasped her hands together. "Are you kidding me?"

"Nope," he said. "We can't be the only ones dancing." Even though she was the only one in the room who mattered to him tonight.

"I love y...it," she said before the ladies all gathered together in a circle, with greetings and hugs.

The guys, being guys, made a beeline for the punch.

"There anything in here besides 7UP and pomegranate juice?" his twin asked.

"I think you'll enjoy the kick," Nick said before embracing his brother.

Morgan stared at Nick for a long moment. "I can't believe this day has come."

"It's too early to celebrate," Nick said. "Not a done deal yet."

"Fair enough," Morgan said before turning to their cousin Grayson. "Never a better time for a toast."

Grayson smiled and nodded. "Couldn't agree more."

The pair went to work pouring drinks into clear cups as the other stood around and talked.

The DJ took his station before welcoming everyone. He kicked off the event with one of Vanessa's favorite dance songs, *I Wanna Dance With Somebody,* by Whitney Houston.

NICK: Firebrand Cowboys

Nick polished off his drink, set the empty cup on the table, and took the cue to walk over to Vanessa when he caught her glance over at him and smile.

"May I have this dance?" he asked as she took a step away from the circle.

"I thought you'd never ask," she said. He had another question, but it could wait until he steeled his nerves.

An hour went by in a flash, dancing despite the boot and laughing. It was the best time Nick had had in longer than he could remember. He'd been to parties before. This one was special because of Vanessa. She lit up the room with her smile. Her eyes danced with excitement and joy like he'd never seen before.

When the DJ played, *I Will Always Love You,* by her favorite artist, he knew it was time. After the slow dance stopped, he signaled the DJ to hold off on the next song.

Nick brought his hands up to cup Vanessa's face. "You're beautiful."

"So are you," she said with the kind of twinkle in her eyes that signaled he was in a whole heap of trouble with this woman.

Everything was perfect in this moment, looking into those eyes of her. So, he took her hands in his, bent down on one knee with some effort, and looked up at her.

The pure look of shock had him almost thinking twice about asking the question, but his heart would never forgive him if he chickened out now. She could say no if she wanted, but he had to know if she felt the same way.

Suddenly, the room shrank to two people. And he knew. It was now or never.

"I've been in love with you for twenty years and didn't know it," he started, catching her gaze and holding onto it. "This thing between us started when we were just kids and had no idea what to do with it. But we're not teenagers anymore. I think I've loved you from the minute we first met next to the pool. What I didn't know was that I wouldn't find anyone who even came close to you for the next two decades."

Vanessa bit down on her bottom lip.

"This time, I don't want to let you go," he said. "Because if you walk out of my life the second time, I'll lose you forever. I love you, Vanessa. Heart and soul. And I would be honored if you would agree to marry me."

He produced a ring box from his jacket pocket.

"Vanessa Mosely, this is me, Nick Firebrand asking you to be my wife."

He opened the box.

"I'm not sure why it took us so long to get here, Nick Firebrand, but I've loved you almost my whole life," Vanessa said. "You're the most brave, honest, intelligent man I've ever met or ever will. So, yes, I'll marry you. Because I lost you once and I would not survive losing you again."

"It's a good thing you'll never have to find out and neither will I," Nick said as he took the diamond solitaire out of the box and then slipped it on her finger.

Then, he stood up and kissed his soon-to-be bride.

The sounds of whoops and cheers filled the room. He heard the pop of champagne corks. And then he was handed two cups, one he gave to Vanessa.

"To this beautiful lady who has agreed to be my wife," he said, raising a glass.

His brothers and cousins all gave toasts. Sharing this moment with family was all he needed to make it perfect. Except for one thing.

Someone was waiting outside.

"Hold on for just a moment," he said to Vanessa.

Confusion knitted her eyebrows but she didn't question him.

He hobbled over to the double doors where a female figure waited, opened them. "She said yes."

Vanessa's mother smiled before wiping away tears. "I always thought it was a shame the two of you didn't end up together. You had the kind of connection that doesn't come around but once in a lifetime."

"We found each other again," he said. "That's all that matters."

"Agreed."

"Now, come see your daughter," he said, wishing his own mother could be present. Morgan had agreed to video the proposal, so Nick could show her at his next visitation.

"Mom?" Vanessa asked in disbelief.

"I've missed you so much," Renee Mosely, now Renee Hastings, said.

"Me too, Mama," Vanessa said, pulling her mother into an embrace. "You make the celebration complete."

The two hugged for a long moment. Then, Renee pulled back and said, "If this is truly a celebration, I'm going to need some champagne."

"Coming up," Nick said, his heart full. He had everything he needed right here in this room. If Vanessa ever changed her mind about having kids, he would do that too.

Whatever made her happy. Because she was everything to him and he planned to spend the rest of his life making sure she knew.

18

EPILOGUE

Standing on the edge of the Rio Grande National Forest, Rowan Firebrand powered up his cell to check messages one more time. Part of taking time off meant going off the grid. He had all the camping gear one needed to truly escape for a while. During much of his trip, he wouldn't have cell coverage. Saving battery meant keeping the phone off unless there was an emergency. He had one portable power pack, just in case he needed the extra charge.

However, he didn't intend to need or use either one. After everything that had happened, he had to get away to find his bearings again. A few weeks of solitude in the forest should do the trick.

Rowan's cell was old and the screen was cracked but it still got the job done. As it turned out, phones, back pockets, and saddles weren't a good mix.

But first, he needed to check his messages. The group chat had blown up over the past few days. Rowan scrolled through, skimming each one.

The phone pinged in his hand. Reading the text

almost stopped his heart. An SOS from Nick. Without hesitating, he pulled up his brother's name from his contacts and tapped the small phone icon to make the call.

"Rowan?" Nick answered, sounding surprised.

"Where are you?" Rowan asked.

"I'm at the house. Why?"

"I just got a text from you with the emergency signal," Rowan explained.

"Oh, right," Nick said. "All good now. I sent that days ago."

"My phone was off," Rowan admitted.

"Does this mean you're coming home?" Nick asked, a hopeful quality to his voice.

"No," Rowan said. "I'm just getting started on my camping trip."

"On your own?"

"Yes," Rowan said. "Just the way I prefer."

"We have a whole lot of open acreage here in Texas," Nick continued without missing a beat.

"Not a hundred and eighty million acres," Rowan quipped. "But this is about getting away from everything Firebrand."

"Colorado does that for you?" Nick asked.

"It does," Rowan confirmed. He started to explain how much easier it was to breathe being far away from the family name.

"I get it," Nick said before Rowan could chime in with his reasoning. "I'm happy for you."

"Is Mom okay?" Rowan asked after thanking his brother.

"Good enough," Nick said. Rowan understood. She was healing while awaiting trial. "Looks like she'll be moved to somewhere safer."

"That's good," Rowan said. "As long as you're alright, I better head out."

"Do you know where you're going?" Nick asked. His brother had to know what Rowan would say even if he did know, which he didn't other than a general idea.

"I'll be alright," Rowan offered, figuring Nick wasn't asking the real question on his mind. "It'll be good to clear my head."

"It's probably for the best," Nick agreed but there was no real conviction in his voice. Rowan was relieved his brother wasn't in trouble.

"I'm going offline for a while," Rowan said. "Not sure how long."

"Thanks for letting me know," Nick said. "I'll send a message to everyone unless you want to."

"I've already done that," Rowan explained. "I just got your SOS text before going dark. Needed to know my brother was okay."

"It's appreciated," Nick said warmly. "Will you be back in time for my wedding?"

"You're what?" Rowan asked, shocked by the announcement.

"Me and Vanessa," he said.

"Mosely?"

"That's right," Nick said. "We found our way back to each other."

"If you make a joke about something being in the water at the ranch, I'm never coming home," Rowan teased, still trying to process the latest development in a long line of changes in his family. A song lyric came to mind, *another one bites the dust.*

"You won't hear it from me," Nick said, "but I wouldn't trust the tap around here."

"You couldn't resist."

"Nope," Nick mused. It was good to hear him sound so happy. Hell, the number of grumpy singles in the family was dissipating faster than rainwater on a Texas sidewalk in summer after the sun came out.

"Take care of yourself while I'm gone," Rowan said, only half joking. His brother sounded better than ever but he'd been through a lot recently and needed time to heal based on the messages in the group chat.

"I was about to say the same to you."

Rowan said goodbye to his brother before ending the call. He could tick all the boxes now. Freedom was waiting as soon as he powered off his cell and headed up the trail. He had everything he needed to survive.

Rucksack strapped onto his back, he tucked his cell into a pocket before zipping it up. And then he headed into the forest.

Keep reading to find out if Rowan finds the peace of mind he's searching for or if the forest holds a dangerous secret that might just kill him. Click here.

ALSO BY BARB HAN

Texas Firebrand

Rancher to the Rescue

Disarming the Rancher

Rancher under Fire

Rancher on the Line

Undercover with the Rancher

Rancher in Danger

Set-Up with the Rancher

Rancher Under the Gun

Taking Cover with the Rancher

Firebrand Cowboys

VAUGHN: Firebrand Cowboys

RAFE: Firebrand Cowboys

MORGAN: Firebrand Cowboys

NICK: Firebrand Cowboys

ROWAN: Firebrand Cowboys

Don't Mess With Texas Cowboys

Texas Cowboy's Protection

Texas Cowboy Justice

Texas Cowboy's Honor

Texas Cowboy Daddy

Texas Cowboy's Baby

Texas Cowboy's Bride

Texas Cowboy's Family

Texas Cowboy Sheriff

Texas Cowboy Marshal

Texas Cowboy Lawman

Texas Cowboy Officer

Texas Cowboy K9 Patrol

Cowboys of Cattle Cove

Cowboy Reckoning

Cowboy Cover-up

Cowboy Retribution

Cowboy Judgment

Cowboy Conspiracy

Cowboy Rescue

Cowboy Target

Cowboy Redemption

Cowboy Intrigue

Cowboy Ransom

For more of Barb's books, visit www.BarbHan.com.

ABOUT THE AUTHOR

Barb Han is a USA TODAY and Publisher's Weekly Bestselling Author. Reviewers have called her books "heartfelt" and "exciting."

Barb lives in Texas—her true north—with her adventurous family, a poodle mix, and a spunky rescue who is often referred to as a hot mess. She is the proud owner of too many books (if there is such a thing). When not writing, she can be found exploring new cities, on a mountain either hiking or skiing depending on the season, or swimming in her own backyard.

Sign up for Barb's newsletter at www.BarbHan.com.